"I met your bride today."

Ryan nearly winced, caught himself just in time and managed to croak out, "Oh, yeah?"

"She seems…sweet."

He caught the pause, found himself meeting Jorie's gaze despite his resolve. She'd put her hair up. It made her cheekbones look high and sexy, like a damn lingerie model.

"I take it you were expecting overbearing and ostentatious."

To his surprise, she appeared to consider the question, her head tipping to the side.

"I don't know what I was expecting," Jorie admitted, her pretty blue eyes narrowing for a moment. "But she's really nice."

Everyone loved Laurel, including the man who'd gotten her pregnant—or so he claimed. He'd run out on her the moment he'd discovered she was pregnant.

"She's a good girl."

Something sparked in Jorie's gaze, something that made him instantly regret his words. Damn it. She was too smart. _____ attraction. Had _____ detail about his wedd_____ now? Had she someh_____ t love his bride?

Dear Reader,

I can't tell you how thrilled I am to bring you *The Rancher's Bride*, my ninth book for Harlequin American Romance. I know I probably shouldn't say this, but I love this book. I really do hate to admit that, too, because it's like proclaiming I love one of my children more than another.

Here's the thing…

Once in a while I'll write a story that calls to me when I'm away from the keyboard. You probably know the feeling well. You find yourself thinking about a book while you're at work, or driving down the road, or out shopping…a bubble of excitement building in your belly as you wonder what will happen next, and if things will all work out, and you Just. Can't. Wait. To. Read. I know it sounds strange, but that's the same sort of feeling I got while writing this book. It doesn't happen all the time, so when it does, I know I'm doing something right.

I laughed. I cried. I wrote the last page and sighed. I sincerely hope, from the bottom of my heart, you experience the same type of emotions while reading the story. And now I hope I haven't doomed you to disappointment.

Thank you for being one of my readers. Thank you for sticking with me through nine books. Thank you for giving me a reason to get up early and stay up late—all in the hopes of bringing you a story like *The Rancher's Bride*.

Pamela

The Rancher's Bride

PAMELA BRITTON

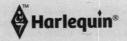

TORONTO NEW YORK LONDON
AMSTERDAM PARIS SYDNEY HAMBURG
STOCKHOLM ATHENS TOKYO MILAN MADRID
PRAGUE WARSAW BUDAPEST AUCKLAND

If you purchased this book without a cover you should be aware
that this book is stolen property. It was reported as "unsold and
destroyed" to the publisher, and neither the author nor the
publisher has received any payment for this "stripped book."

Recycling programs
for this product may
not exist in your area.

ISBN-13: 978-0-373-75411-3

THE RANCHER'S BRIDE

Copyright © 2012 by Pamela Britton

All rights reserved. Except for use in any review, the reproduction or
utilization of this work in whole or in part in any form by any electronic,
mechanical or other means, now known or hereafter invented, including
xerography, photocopying and recording, or in any information storage
or retrieval system, is forbidden without the written permission of the
publisher, Harlequin Enterprises Limited, 225 Duncan Mill Road,
Don Mills, Ontario M3B 3K9, Canada.

This is a work of fiction. Names, characters, places and incidents are
either the product of the author's imagination or are used fictitiously,
and any resemblance to actual persons, living or dead, business
establishments, events or locales is entirely coincidental.

This edition published by arrangement with Harlequin Books S.A.

For questions and comments about the quality of this book
please contact us at Customer_eCare@Harlequin.ca

® and TM are trademarks of the publisher. Trademarks indicated with
® are registered in the United States Patent and Trademark Office, the
Canadian Trade Marks Office and in other countries.

www.Harlequin.com

Printed in U.S.A.

ABOUT THE AUTHOR

With over a million books in print, Pamela Britton likes to call herself the best-known author nobody's ever heard of. Of course, that changed thanks to a certain licensing agreement with that little racing organization known as NASCAR.

But before the glitz and glamour of NASCAR, Pamela wrote books that were frequently voted the best of the best by the *Detroit Free Press,* Barnes & Noble (two years in a row) and *RT Book Reviews.* She's won numerous awards, including the National Reader's Choice Award and a nomination for the Romance Writers of America's Golden Heart.

When not writing books, Pamela is a reporter for a local newspaper. She's also a columnist for *The American Quarter Horse Journal. The Rancher's Bride* is the author's twenty-seventh title.

Books by Pamela Britton
HARLEQUIN AMERICAN ROMANCE
 985—COWBOY LESSONS
1040—COWBOY TROUBLE
1122—COWBOY M.D.
1143—COWBOY VET
1166—COWGIRL'S CEO
1285—THE WRANGLER
1322—MARK, SECRET COWBOY
1373—RANCHER AND PROTECTOR

HQN BOOKS
DANGEROUS CURVES
IN THE GROOVE
ON THE EDGE
TO THE LIMIT
TOTAL CONTROL
ON THE MOVE

For Melissa, sister of my heart, fellow horsey-person extraordinaire, maker of the always divine venison Swiss steak (eat your heart out, Pioneer Woman), consumer of all things martini (with me).
I love you.

Chapter One

The hot breath of Texas enveloped Jorie Peters like a steamy wet blanket.

"Ugh." She grimaced, swiping at a brow already covered by sweat.

So this *was Texas?*

Her gaze swept over rolling hills and grass-covered pastures. It didn't look a thing like she expected.

She inhaled a deep breath of resignation. The scent of fresh-cut grass made the humidity seem heavier. The building she'd parked in front of was filled to the brim with hay and at least four stories tall. Its dark shadow spread across the gravel road like a blob of ink. Three other outbuildings surrounded her. Farm buildings, she clarified—one to her right which held tractors and one to her left which housed equipment, and some kind of long one out in the distance behind the building where she'd parked. She turned, her heel grinding into the gravel as she spun in place, wondering where to go. There was nothing that looked like a horse barn in sight.

"You can't park there."

Her heart jumped out of her throat. She turned, trying to find the voice's owner.

"I have another squeeze of hay coming in."

The words echoed, so much so that she couldn't determine where they came from.

"Up here."

Oh. *Up.*

Her gaze drifted along the hundreds of hay bales. And there he was, at least twenty feet above her, a tall, lanky male wearing an off-white cowboy hat. Well, this was Texas after all, and so she should expect the hat. She was a long ways away from Atlanta. He wore chaps, too—kind of. They were too short for him, the leather flaps looking as if they belonged on a six-year-old and not a grown man. She watched as he began to hop down, navigating the uneven blocks like a billy goat, and when he stopped in front of her, all she could think was *holy moly.*

He looked like something out of a Hanes underwear commercial.

Boxers? Or briefs?

Dark, dark hair. Eyes the color of the Aegean Sea, the stormy kind of sea pirates sailed upon. Or maybe it was his dark good looks that made her think of pirates. He had rough stubble on his chin, and she had a feeling that by five o'clock he'd have quite a shadow on his jawline.

"You should park in front of the barn." His tone was stern.

"That's what I'm looking for." She swiped hair that was quickly turning into a corkscrew of blond curls off her forehead. She'd drawn her hair back into a bun—more professional that way—but as always, several strands had escaped. She was probably a mess after her twelve-hour drive. No doubt she had as much dust on her as her compact car. "I was told there was an office upstairs and that I should see Odelia Clayborne."

He swiped some sweat off his forehead, the motion allowing a better glimpse of his eyes. They were piercing. Truly amazing.

"You Jorie Peters?" His gaze swept over her black business suit and what suddenly seemed like a silly choice of shoes—black pumps.

"I am," she said in surprise.

"Barn's over there." He motioned with his chin, turning away as if about to climb the hay bales once more.

"You mean the big long building?" she called out after him.

He nodded, half turned. He smelled of hard work, the tangy scent of man catching a wayward breeze and drifting over to her. It reminded her that it'd been a long time since…well, just since.

"The really big building over there," he explained. "It's a covered arena. One with stalls inside and an office upstairs."

Ah. That explained it. She'd been looking for her own idea of a horse stable. Red. Double doors. One with a white *X* painted on the front.

The sound of a tractor caught her attention. His, too. They both turned.

"Better move that car," he ordered, pointing as if she needed help identifying her vehicle.

Jorie immediately saw why. A huge stack of hay was headed in their direction, one propelled by a tractor of some sort, the driver's cab completely obscured by the grassy blocks.

Good heavens, how did the driver see?

"Thanks," she shouted as she all but dove for her car. That was all she needed—a tractor to run over her Honda.

Her only possession.

She slid inside her vehicle, refusing to think about that. This was a new start. A new life. Her business in Georgia—Wedding Belles—was now defunct. A victim of the recession, just as she was herself. In her rearview mirror she caught a glimpse of the cowboy, the man watching her take off, hands on his hips.

Jerk.

No smiles. No words of welcome. Just "move your car."

How did he know who she was?

Whatever. She had more important matters on her mind, like meeting her new boss.

Jorie steered her vehicle past one of the outbuildings, immediately spotting a house in the distance to her left that'd been blocked from her view, although calling it a house seemed like a misnomer. The place would have done *Gone with the Wind* proud. Three stories tall. Four white columns that sprouted up from a wraparound porch, and dark green shutters on either side of the windows…and there were a lot of windows. A porch swing hung between two of the columns. Rattan furniture was clustered near the corner of the rail. Behind the house a line of trees could be seen a few hundred yards away. Jorie wondered if there was a creek down there. It sure looked like it.

"Wow."

The oaks were huge, their shiny foliage a darker green than the grassy hills that surrounded them. Behind the mansion was another house, smaller, but just as beautiful.

Was that the bridal suite, the one her new boss had told her about? The place where brides were pampered in the hours leading up to their weddings? Masseuse, manicurist, hair stylist—all brought in from the outside to make their day special. And not just brides, but the bridesmaids, too.

The road forked. She took the branch to her right.

Spring Hill Ranch was not what she expected.

For some reason she'd been thinking single-story buildings, white picket fences, maybe a rustic-looking barn. This place looked like a movie set. Sure, off in the distance were the white fences—she'd followed one down a long, sweeping driveway for what must have been at least a mile—but this place was a private sanctuary that took Jorie's breath away. No wonder brides flocked to the location to get married. She could picture a carriage rolling down the hills to a wedding tent pitched beneath a grove of trees.

"Here we go," she said as she pulled up in front of yet another strange-looking building. This one had a massive opening in the front. Inside she spotted a horse and a rider, the pair galloping around so fast it was a wonder the man's hat didn't fall off.

Her door creaked when she slammed it closed, something that'd been happening more and more of late. With over 100,000 miles on the odometer it was a wonder the car had made it to Texas.

"Hello?" she called out to the rider.

It wasn't a cowboy.

It was a cowgirl—or maybe cow-*woman* was a better description. The rider had gray hair, the light blue shirt she wore clinging to a trim body that belied her age. She skidded to a stop, literally, her horse leaving twin tracks in the arena dust.

"Jorie?" the woman called out in surprise.

She was at least twenty feet from her, and yet her vision must have been sharp, especially since the arena was set back from the entrance. Jorie slipped inside the building through a massive opening. It was at least twenty degrees cooler inside.

"Mrs. Clayborne?"

Even though her eyes were still adjusting to the darkness inside, Jorie could see the woman's teeth flash.

"Why, you *are* Jorie, aren't you?" the woman said, her southern accent catching on vowels and elongating them.

She wore chaps, too, and they were as short as the ones worn by the man in the hay barn, only these had fringe and silver conchos up the side. Beneath the chocolate-brown leather she wore jeans, and tucked into those jeans was a fancy Western shirt complete with white fringe along the front that complemented the woman's light eyes and gray hair.

"My goodness. I didn't expect you for another day." The woman jumped down from her brown horse as if she were twenty rather than the sixty Jorie judged her to be. A horse neighed, and Jorie spotted a row of fancy stalls on the other side of the piped fencing that encircled the arena.

She'd driven straight through. Barely stopping to use the rest room in Louisiana, Jorie was ashamed to admit that she hadn't had the money to spend yet another night in a hotel.

"I was anxious to get here."

The woman clucked, her horse's neck stretching out as it reluctantly followed behind. The closer she came to Jorie, the more the tension in Jorie's shoulders eased. The woman's eyes were a balm to Jorie's battered soul. They were kind, unlike that cowboy's eyes.

"Well, I'm glad you made it, honey." She patted the neck of her horse. "You must be exhausted."

That was an understatement. She hadn't had sleep in,

well, in a while. She'd passed the point of being hungry, too. All she wanted was a bed.

"Why don't I get Ryan to show you to your quarters?" She opened a gate, the metal catch clanking and echoing across the arena. The horse she led, an animal with a brown body and a black mane and tail, snorted. "He's my son." She flashed another smile.

And Jorie put it all together. Actually, she should have realized it the moment she looked into the woman's eyes. They were the same color. Only it was hard to fathom the two of them being related. The woman in front of her had a generous smile and kind eyes, while her son had...well, suffice it to say the apple had fallen *far* from this tree.

"Come on. I'll introduce you two."

"I think he's unloading hay."

"Did you see him?" the woman asked, motioning Jorie to follow as they headed down a wide aisle along the front of the building and toward the row of stalls. Jorie noticed her hat then, fancy stitching embroidered into the brim. Some kind of floral design with rhinestone crystals in the middle.

Pretty.

"Actually, I think we've already met."

The woman stopped, gray brows lifting nearly to the brim of her hat. "Oh?"

"He's the one who told me where the barn was."

"Ah," the woman said, as though given the key to a great mystery, at least judging by the expression on her face. "And I'm sure he was his usual charming self."

That was an understatement.

"Don't mind him." Her new boss smirked a bit as she shook her head. "He hates how my idea has taken off. Thinks it's silly. Can't stand sharing the ranch with a bunch of spoiled brides, as he calls them. Claims it's a pain in the butt to be dealing with a steady stream of visitors."

"Move your car."

Yeah, she could see that.

"We have a wedding coming up and he always gets a little cranky beforehand."

"Good to know."

"Calls it the 'invasion of Normandy.'" The woman looked heavenward in mock dismay. "Come on." Jorie felt something nudge her shoulder, and she eyed the horse warily. She wasn't a big fan of the animals, not that she'd had a whole lot of interaction with them in Georgia.

"We'll take your car up there. That way you can park it out in front of your new apartment," Odelia said. "Let me put Chex away."

Her own apartment. A place to live. A monthly salary. Financial security. It was why she'd driven hundreds of miles to go to work for a woman she'd never met, all in the hope of taking Odelia's little "hobby" to the next level. The reason she would suck it up and make nice to her new boss's son, even though she suspected she and this Ryan guy would never get along.

"I'm so glad you've met him," Odelia was saying.

"Um, yeah. Me, too."

"The two of you needed to make each other's acquaintance."

As long as she got to keep her distance from here on out, they'd get along just fine.

"Especially since the two of you will be sharing an office."

Jorie stumbled.

Odelia must have seen her surprise. "Oh, don't worry." She gave Jorie a wide smile. "His bark is worse than his bite."

Chapter Two

Ryan heard them coming before he saw them.

"I guess you were right, boss."

Ryan glanced at Sam, who leaned against the cab of the squeeze he'd been driving, a smirk on his face. Sam had worked for them since he was fourteen years old, and he knew Ryan's mother about as well as he knew his own, which meant he knew Odelia's latest hobby drove Ryan nuts.

"Damn," Ryan muttered. He'd been hoping for at least a day of peace and quiet. He still had to drag the arena, disc the back pasture and fix a whole host of other little things that were the bane of his existence. Then there were his mom's little wedding guest fixes. Oil the hinges on the gate so they didn't squeak. Fix a broken sash in the "bridal cottage." Dump a load of gravel in one of the potholes so wedding guests wouldn't "bounce."

God help him.

Sam must have read the expression on his face because he chuckled. "I guess she's pretty serious about this little venture of hers, huh?" Sam was three-quarters Cherokee, but he didn't need a sixth sense to know Ryan's mom had gone insane.

Ten years ago it'd been floral arrangements. Ryan

would bet she'd created memorial bouquets for half the county's deceased. From there she'd moved on to stained glass. That hadn't lasted too long, something about being too clumsy, thank God. Antiques had been next. He'd gotten to the point that he refused to go anywhere with her. To this day he couldn't drive past an estate sale without cringing. Now it was weddings.

Weddings.

He wished to the good Lord above that he knew who'd put such a stupid idea in his mother's head. If he ever found out, he'd drag the person behind a horse. For six months he'd been putting up with uptight brides, cranky mamas and wedding guests who'd never been on a real working ranch. But the most shocking thing of all, the thing that really had him twisted up in knots, was that the damn business had taken off. They were completely booked for the rest of the year. And now she'd gone and hired some kind of big-time coordinator. From Georgia.

"We just need to hang in there a little longer," he said. "My mom will get over her obsession."

And that fancy little wedding coordinator could go back to Georgia and his life would return to normal.

"That's what you said three months ago."

"Shut up, Sam."

His friend glanced over at him sharply, laughed, but whatever else he'd been about to say was cut off by the arrival of the same blue compact car as before, only this time his mother was in the passenger seat. On the other side of the windshield he could see her mouth going a hundred miles an hour, typical of his mom. The woman driving was nodding and smiling.

Until she caught sight of him.

The smile dropped from her face like a brick. Okay.

So maybe he'd been a little hard on her earlier. No. Not hard. Unwelcoming. But, damn it, this whole wedding thing was BS.

"You didn't tell me she was smokin' hot."

Ryan didn't need to ask who Sam was talking about. "Doesn't matter what she looks like."

It was true, though. His mom's new wedding coordinator was pretty. She had hair so blond he would have sworn it was from a bottle except he'd looked for the telltale signs: the dark roots, the fake streaks of blond, the black eyebrows. He'd spotted none of those things which meant it might be real. She had the blue eyes to go along with it, too.

"Good thing Laurel's so sweet, else she might be jealous."

Laurel. His fiancée.

"She'll probably welcome her with open arms," he heard himself say before shoving off to greet his mother. He didn't like thinking about Laurel.

His future bride.

He felt a bead of sweat trickle down his brow.

"My, my, my," his mother marveled as she got out of the car. "You finished putting all that hay up in record time." She glanced back at the driver. "Come on out, Jorie. You need to meet Sam."

She was wearing one of her Annie Oakley outfits again. Lord help him. She'd never dressed like that before, but lately she'd been wearing the fringed shirts and fancy Western hats as if they lived in some kind of theme park—and maybe they did. His mom had told him time and time again that city people loved their ranch because of the ambience. That must be why she'd been channeling the ghost of Westerns past.

"Not quite," Ryan said. "We've still got one more load to go."

"Well, that can wait." She hooked an arm through her new employee's. "Jorie, this is Sam."

"Nice to meet you, ma'am." The two shook hands, Sam going so far as to tip his hat.

Ryan smirked. Leave it to Sam to try and charm a woman he'd just met.

"And this is my son, Ryan, whom I think you already met. Ryan, Jorie here is exhausted. Why don't you hop in her car and drive her down to her quarters. She has luggage she needs unloaded, too."

He didn't shake her hand, just nodded, not that she noticed.

"Oh, that's not necessary," the blonde interjected. As he had earlier, he noticed the black suit she wore accentuated the shape of her body, something he definitely shouldn't be aware of given that he was engaged. "I can unload my own suitcase."

"Nonsense," his mother said with a pat to the woman's arm. "You need your rest. I hate to say it, dear, but you look plumb wore out."

His mother was right. Though she had a flawless complexion, she appeared pale, her pretty blue eyes glazed by a sheen of fatigue.

"Come on," he said, taking pity on the woman against his better judgment. He motioned her toward her car.

She didn't move.

Stubborn, huh?

She glared.

Ooo. And she had claws. This might be fun, after all.

"Go on," his mother ordered.

She met Ryan's gaze again, her blue eyes narrowing.

"You heard my mother," he said. "Go on."

Clearly, she wanted to argue. Just as clearly, she wanted to please. She turned, reluctance personified. Ryan almost smiled, but he was too busy noticing her legs. He couldn't tell if she wore panty hose or not, but she sure had some tan legs…and shapely.

Cut it out.

"I can drive," he heard her say as he headed to the driver's side

"I won't hear of any such thing," his mom answered for him. "Ryan will drive you. Sam, why don't you go get that last squeeze of hay. I'll guide it in."

"Don't be ridiculous, Mom." Ryan stripped his gloves off and tucked them in his back pocket before opening the passenger-side door. "I'll finish up just as soon as I drive Ms. Peters here to her new quarters."

The woman had reluctantly slid into the seat, the door closing with a heavy thud.

"You're a good son." His mother came around the side of the car, reached up and patted his cheek—just before kissing him—as if he were seven years old and not thirty.

But despite the irritation he felt at being treated like a child, he couldn't deny one thing: he loved his mom. She might be a pain in his rear, but she was the only family he had.

He opened the driver's side door, the smell of perfume or floral shampoo instantly enveloping him.

He nearly closed his eyes.

Now, the woman in the car? She was going to be a pain in his rear, too, he could tell.

He didn't like her.

Jorie leaned back in the passenger seat and closed her eyes, so exhausted she felt as if she could go to sleep right then and there. Except she couldn't. Not with *him* in the car.

"Buckle up," was all he said.

Cool currents from the car's air conditioner wafted across Jorie's face as he put the car in gear, but it wasn't enough to drown out the smell of him. He stank.

No, he doesn't.

He smells *manly.*

Be nice to him, Jorie. He's your boss's son.

Jorie forced her eyes open, shot him a glance. He was as muscular as a professional athlete.

"Do you play football?"

Stupid, stupid, *ridiculous* thing to ask. What was wrong with her?

He'd glanced over at her as if she had tentacles hanging from her ears.

"Huh?" He drove her car between the two farm buildings, his eyes quickly bouncing between her and the gravel road.

"Never mind," she said. Darn it. Why did she always do that? A thought would pop into her head and, bam, out it came.

"Ah, no," he said, having obviously figured out what she'd said. "I've never played football."

Just pretend like you meant to ask the question, Jorie.

"Your mom seems nice," she said next.

"She's a pain in the butt."

"Excuse me?"

"I'm thinking about having her committed to an old folk's home."

"You are not."

"I even called a couple places, but they wouldn't

take her just yet. I have to wait until her dementia gets a little more advanced."

"Dementia?" Jorie asked, sitting up in her seat.

And then he smiled.

He was teasing her.

"Gotcha."

"Why, you little—" She couldn't think what to say, not without insulting him at least, and not as tired as she was.

"Little what?" he prompted.

Okay, so he wasn't just good-looking. He was drop-dead gorgeous. And, apparently, he had a sense of humor.

"You're not very nice."

"Sorry. Thought I should try to break the ice."

He drove her car down a gently sloping hillside, and Jorie was presented with a vista that took her breath away. A pasture lay spread out in front of her. To the right was an old barn, to her left another grove of trees, one with two homes nearby. The same creek she'd noticed earlier was here, too, tall oak trees surrounded yet another group of homes.

"What do you think?" he asked.

"It's lovely," she said.

"That used to be the main homestead," he explained. The tires crunched as he took a fork to the left. "The barn over to our right is what my mom lovingly calls the 'wedding chapel.'"

She'd seen pictures of it on the internet, but Jorie made a mental note to suggest adding a photo page to Spring Hill Ranch's website, one that would highlight the rustic charm of their venue. The rolling hills and stately trees were just stunning.

Seconds later he pulled to a stop in front of one of

the homes, a charming single-story with wood window-panes and a tiny front porch.

"You'll be living in a home that used to belong to the ranch foreman, only that's me these days, so I live in the main house right there." He pointed to a home about four-hundred yards away. "The *old* main house. My mom lives in the big one over the hill."

"You mean you'll be living next door to me?"

He shut off the car. "Yup. And I'll be giving you a ride to our office every day, too."

Our office.

She'd completely forgotten about that.

Suddenly there didn't seem to be enough air in the vehicle.

He's turned off the car, you dork.

"Look," he said, pulling her keys out. "I don't mean to rain on your parade, but I feel I should tell you something." He fiddled with her keys a second. "My mom," he said. "She goes through these…phases. Over the years she's tried a number of things."

She saw him frown, and even in profile he was handsome. "Look, I know you just drove all the way out here from Georgia, but things might change, you know? My mom's the best mom in the world, but she gets burrs up her butt from time to time. Like this wedding thing. I'd hate for you to have turned down a lucrative job in Georgia for something that might be temporary."

Lucrative? In Georgia?

And *temporary?*

"Are you saying I've made a mistake?"

"No, no," he said quickly. "That's not what I meant at all. I just think you should be prepared, you know, in case things don't work out."

He *was* telling her not to unpack her bags.

"I appreciate your concern," she said, and she had no doubt he heard the frost in her voice. "But I'm a big girl, one who can take care of herself."

"No, I think you've misunderstood—"

"I understand perfectly," she contradicted, leaving the car before she said something else, something that really *would* get her fired from her job.

"Wait." He got out of the car, too. "You'll need this."

He tossed her something. She caught it. A key, although where he'd gotten it from, she didn't know.

"Thanks," she said.

"I'll leave your luggage on the porch."

She nodded, turning toward her new home. Her hands shook in anger. How dare he try to ruin this for her? Didn't he realize she had nowhere else to go? No job back in Georgia. No home. This was the end of the road for her.

"Welcome to Spring Hill Ranch," he called out after her.

She turned on her heel, a descriptive word, one that wasn't very flattering, hanging off the tip of her tongue.

"Thank you," she said, lifting her chin up in challenge. "I plan on being here for a very, *very* long time."

He stared at her for what seemed like an eternity. Something that resembled admiration filled his eyes, but she must be imagining that.

"Good for you," she thought she heard him say.

She held his gaze for another moment before turning away.

Jerk.

Chapter Three

She must sleep like the dead, Ryan thought, shifting the quiche his mom had baked for Jorie and knocking on the front door yet again.

"Damn it, Mom," he muttered, glancing in the general direction of where she lived. Why did she always have him do her dirty work? The last thing he needed was to play delivery boy.

He turned away, quiche still in hand, and headed for the steps, only to halt again. His mom would kill him if he didn't do as asked.

"Shoot."

A thin sliver of pink light outlined the small hill that blocked his view of his mom's house. Dawn. It had just arrived, the sky still dark behind him. He had a million things to do today. Cows to gather. A meeting at nine. Errands to run. The last thing he needed to do was play nursemaid to his mother's new employee.

"'You go check on her in the morning,'" he mimicked. "'Give her my quiche. Make sure she's all right.'"

He glanced heavenward.

"Man, it's a good thing I love you, Mom."

He turned back to the door. To be fair, he hadn't seen his mom's new employee since dropping off her luggage, something he'd told his mother last night, and something that concerned him just a little bit. He thought about leaving the quiche on the porch, but one of the ranch dogs would no doubt find it, and he could just imagine what his mom would do if one of his dogs ate Jorie's quiche.

"Crap."

He knocked again, louder, and when nothing happened, leaned his ear against the door. Some kind of weird noise came back to him. TV? He stepped to the right, tried to peer through the window that looked into a tiny family room that stretched across the front of the house. Nothing.

"To hell with it."

She'd been asleep for a long time. Time to get up and take this quiche off his hands.

He balanced the pie plate in one hand, the ring of keys he pulled from his pocket jingling as he sought to unlock the door.

This is a bad idea.

It's what his mom would want him to do.

You're breaking into her house.

It's not her *house,* he told himself firmly, pushing the door open a crack.

Just set the damn quiche down and go.

But then he heard the noise again, a horrendous sound that put him instantly on alert. It was as dark as a haunted house inside, the sun not yet high enough to send even ambient light through the windows. He paused for a moment, listening...and there it went again.

Snoring.

He felt a gust of laughter, despite his ire. *That's* what he'd heard?

Okay. She's fine. Just leave the quiche on the side table.

Yet his curiosity got the better of him. These weren't tiny little ladylike squeaks. These were rip-snorting, drapery-rustling, window-vibrating breaths, and he could only imagine how loud they must be if he could hear them all the way through the front door. Against his better judgment he found himself moving forward.

The ranch home was easy to navigate, the shape of it a simple square: kitchen at the back of the house to his left, bedroom across the hall from it and to the right, and the open area in the front where he stood.

His eyes had started to adjust, making him realize that it wasn't quite so dark anymore. A pale pink glow slid through the window at the end of the hall allowing for light to dribble onto the hardwood floors. Ambient light also spilled in her bedroom windows, which was how he spied the snoring, sleeping goddess that lay sprawled amidst tumbled sheets like a magazine centerfold.

He almost dropped the pie plate.

Okay, so maybe not naked, but close enough in her mini white tank top and matching skimpy underwear. She lay on her side, a quilt made of red and pink squares wound between her legs and around her torso. Yesterday he'd wondered if she wore panty hose. Today he realized she was tan all over, her calves, her thighs, even the tiny sliver of skin he glimpsed between the triangle of her bikini underwear and the quilt. The blond hair he'd admired yesterday lay around her, mussed, yet no less beautiful in the morning light. She had the softest looking skin, her cheeks naturally tinted a pale pink, her lips thick and generous.

And then she gobbled down a gust of air, the sound she shot out causing Ryan to flinch. If he'd been a dog, he'd have tilted his head.

Good Lord.

How could something so gorgeous make a sound that was loud enough to wake the dead? The noise reverberated through the room, and even in the morning light he could see her frown—as if bothered by the fact that the noise disturbed her sleep.

He smiled. How did she not wake up?

But now that he'd solved the mystery it was time to get the hell out, he told himself, starting to back away. He'd forgotten the pie, however, and had to dash back to the kitchen to set it down. On the way out his foot hit something, a something that made a noise as it began to fall.

His mind registered that it was a broom and he tried to catch it, but it fell to the ground with a clatter.

Get out.

He shot toward the door as though a herd of rabid squirrels were on his heels. Behind him the snoring had abruptly stopped. Ryan moved even faster.

Almost there.

His hand hit the door.

She didn't wake up earlier. She wouldn't wake up now?

He began to swing the door open.

"What the hell!"

JORIE CLUTCHED THE bedspread around her, using her elbow to keep everything in place as she blinked and then blinked again.

A man stood in her doorway.

"Who the hell—?"

The man turned back to face her, reluctantly it seemed.

Ryan Clayborne.

"I knocked," he said, managing to sound both nervous and defensive at the same time.

"You let yourself in?" It was taking a moment for her brain to wake up. When she'd first woken up, she'd had to think for a moment where she was because prior to opening her eyes, she'd been having a dream about a man with dark hair—

Nope. Not going *there.*

"My mom. She was worried last night. Wanted me to check on you this morning."

"So you just *let* yourself *in?*" she repeated.

"I heard a noise. And you've been asleep for hours."

But then something he'd just said sank in. Morning? It wasn't morning.

Was it?

She glanced out the window to his left, the parted drapes revealing a seashell-colored sky, one that could signal dusk...or dawn.

And then she heard it. A rooster. It crowed in the distance.

Morning.

She ran a hand through her hair. Her eyes felt gritty. And if she were honest, she felt a little woozy.

"I need to get dressed for work."

"Does your throat hurt?"

Jorie froze. It took a moment for her sleep-numbed mind to absorb his words.

"I've never heard a woman snore like you do." His brows drew together a bit. "Is it a genetic thing?"

"Go away," she said, rubbing her eyes. She'd slept all night? And half an afternoon of the day before. Had she been that exhausted?

Apparently so.

"Maybe you should eat something. I left my mom's quiche on the kitchen table."

"No. I'm fine." She was actually famished, she suddenly realized. "Thanks for waking me up. I'll be dressed in just a minute, but don't wait for me. I can walk to work."

"Work?" Ryan frowned again. "You don't have to work today. You're not slated to start until Monday. It's Friday. Eat your breakfast."

He turned way.

"I'll be at the office in fifteen minutes."

He glanced back at her, his gaze sliding downward, only to pause for a moment. Color bloomed on her cheeks because she could feel cool air on her legs, knew the blanket covered little more than her upper thighs and torso.

"Eat your breakfast," he repeated, that gaze of his doing something, a something that caused her whole body to react in a way that it really shouldn't.

"My mom won't be happy if you don't."

Something flickered, something heated and dark that turned his aqua-colored eyes a deep green.

He turned away again.

She felt the cover slip, and Jorie realized she'd been standing there, gawking....

No, going gooey.

The door closed, bringing her back to earth. She blinked.

Not gooey, just famished. She hadn't had any dinner the night before. No lunch, either. Maybe even not any breakfast.

Quiche.

She hitched the cover up, told herself she'd been

imagining whatever she saw, and strode to the 1960s-style kitchen.

There it was, the quiche, sitting on the table in all its glory, a golden stream of light illuminating its flaky depths as if it was a gift from God.

Not really.

It just seemed that way because she was so damn hungry, and she wanted to scarf that quiche down more than anything she'd ever wanted in her life—her stomach actually growled at the thought.

"To hell with it."

She *would* go to the office. She would eat the quiche later, at her desk.

She turned, thankful that she'd had the foresight to lay out her clothes the night before, because it suddenly became important to catch him before he left.

She washed up and dressed in record time, ran to the floor-length mirror in the corner of the room, checked her appearance to ensure the black slacks and off-white button-down blouse weren't crooked, then ran to the door. She grabbed a brush along the way, all the while listening for the sound of his truck starting up. Nothing. He must have gone to his own house. She almost hurried past the quiche, but she ran back and grabbed the pastry. Maybe she'd eat on the way. No sense in passing out at his feet. She'd use her hands if she had to—

An engine roared to life.

"Wait!" she shouted.

She jammed a finger on the doorknob, cursed, almost dropped the quiche and burst out the front door so fast she left one of her heels behind.

"Damn it."

She darted back to get it, couldn't manage to get her foot in, gave up, kicked the other one off, scooped them both up, and somehow managed to balance her heels, her quiche and her brush the whole time she ran toward his still idling truck.

"Don't go," she called, her loose hair streaming out behind her.

She could see him sitting inside, and then she all but skidded to a stop.

The passenger door was open.

He wasn't about to leave, he was *waiting* for her.

"Son of a—"

He'd known she'd race to catch up to him. Had somehow so anticipated her next move that he now sat in the driver's seat, head leaned back against the headrest, hat tipped low over his closed eyes.

She slowly approached. When she drew near the open door he glanced over at her. "Took you long enough."

Chapter Four

She'd covered those damn sexy legs of hers with slacks.

She would look even better in jeans.

Stop thinking about her legs.

Ryan leaned forward, fixed his hat and put his truck in gear.

"You didn't have to wait."

"No," he said. "I didn't."

He wasn't entirely certain why he *had* waited. He hadn't even been certain she'd really get dressed and head to the office. A lot of people would have taken the opportunity to take the day off, and yet somehow he'd known she wasn't the type.

"Thank you."

He glanced over at her again. She looked ready for church in her no-frills button-down blouse and slacks. Gorgeous without even trying. He liked that about her, liked how she looked with her hair loose. He'd liked the way she'd looked standing before him, too, shapely legs exposed to his view, that frickin' bedspread wrapped around her body as if she was a countrified version of the Statue of Liberty.

Enough.

He rolled his window down, grateful for the fresh

burst of morning air that quickly cooled his overheated cheeks.

Your cheeks aren't the only part that's hot.

"You going to eat that quiche or just stare at it?" he asked as he thrust his truck in reverse.

She did keep peeking glances at it, her tongue flicking out and licking her lower lip as if she was contemplating the idea of simply burying her face into the middle of it.

"I don't have a fork," she said with all the morose sadness of a little girl missing her Barbie doll.

"Use your hands," he said, putting the gearshift into First and mashing down the pedal a little too hard. A couple seconds later they crested the small hill, Ryan glancing toward his mom's house, the one he'd grown up in but had abandoned when he was old enough to want his independence and to bring a woman home. The lights were on in the kitchen, a sure sign she was up, no doubt plotting other ways to make his life hell.

"I can't use my hands."

And despite his sour mood, he found himself on the verge of a chuckle. It wasn't funny, but the way she almost wailed the words sure did tickle his funny bone.

"Maybe you should have stayed at the house, had some breakfast."

She didn't say anything, just looked out the window, and Ryan admitted that she was the prettiest little thing he'd ever seen. Period.

And you're engaged, buddy.

He stepped on the accelerator, racing by the hay barn and tractor shed perhaps a little too fast, but anxious to get to work quickly nonetheless. His tires lost purchase when he stopped in front of the wide opening. Ryan cut off the big diesel engine and jumped out before he could have another wayward thought.

Horses nickered. The sensor-light buzzed on. He heard her truck door open, thought about helping her out of the truck before chastising himself yet again. She wasn't some kind of damn ranch guest. She was his mother's latest implement of torture, one he'd have to babysit until his mom's arrival.

"Stairway to the office is to the left." He flicked the barn lights on, horses nickering again. "Go on up and make yourself at home. Eat some of that quiche."

"Where are you going?"

"Feed the horses." He couldn't resist teasing her. "You want to help?"

Her answer was nearly instantaneous. "No."

Thank God.

"But I probably should."

"What?" He blinked and turned back to her. She was still juggling the quiche and her heels, the cuff of her black slacks dragging on the ground. "What makes you say that?"

"Your mom told me I needed to get comfortable around horses, you know, in case I needed to lead a bride to the altar on a horse or something."

She was serious. "You can save your horse lessons for later."

It was the wrong thing to say, he could tell instantly. She was the type of woman that didn't like to be told what to do, especially by a man. "I'd rather start now."

"You can't feed horses in that outfit."

She glanced down as if surprised by his words. "Why not?"

"You'll get hay all over yourself."

She dropped her heels, slipped her feet in them and

glanced back up at him with a smile. "Nonsense," she said, holding the quiche out in front of her. "I've seen horses fed on TV. It doesn't look very hard. The pitchfork does all the work."

TV? *Pitchfork?*

He almost explained the truth of the matter, but her stubborn I-can-do-anything-you-can-do-better attitude really got on his nerves.

"You can set your quiche down in the tack room," he said, figuring if she wanted an introduction to horses lesson, he'd damn-well-skippy give her one. "Follow me."

Pitchfork. He nearly laughed. Not unless this was circa 1830.

He turned on the light when they reached the tack room, a spacious room at the end of the row of stalls, one that was filled with Western saddles and bridles and smelled of leather and saddle soap. A glance back revealed Jorie standing just outside, one shoe kicked off, left foot out behind her, the woman shaking it as though she was a cat who'd stepped in a pool of water. He almost laughed again. Barn aisle dirt had a way of seeping into heels, or so he'd been told.

"Here." He held his hand out. "I'll set your quiche down right there."

It should be safe from the flash mob otherwise known as Mom's Mutts on the grooming shelf to his right, he thought, dreading the arrival of the gaggle of ranch dogs. People were forever dropping their unwanted pets out in the country, and for some reason they always seemed to gravitate toward the Spring Hill Ranch. They settled in as if the place was some kind of canine retirement home.

"I'll start at one end and you can start on the other."

He guided her to the feed room located next to the tack room. It was double the size of their tack room, double the height, too, with bales of hay stacked to the ceiling. This was horse hay, though, which meant the sweet smell of alfalfa filled the room. "They each get one flake."

"Flake?" She looked perplexed standing there in her designer pants.

"Yup." He went to the closest bale, pulled out his pocket knife, slit the baling twine. It came apart with a pop and a twang, the hay still warm on the inside. They'd just loaded it into the feed room yesterday. "It should be as wide as this." He slipped the knife back in his pocket, held up his hands, and touched his two thumbs together so she could observe the space between them.

"What about the pitchfork?" She glanced around as if looking for one.

He didn't want his lips to twitch with a smile, but they did. "Nobody uses pitchforks to feed horses anymore." He grabbed one of the soft, green flakes. Well, that wasn't precisely true. He supposed some old-timers might still use them, but not here where everything was state-of-the-art.

He brushed by her, pausing for a moment near the door to watch. She approached the bale as if it was a complicated puzzle, reached down, picked up a flake, and then did exactly as he'd thought she'd do as she straightened. She held the thing up to her chest like a giant library book, gasping as stalks of alfalfa slipped right down that fancy shirt of hers.

"Ack."

She dropped the flake of hay, brushing at the front of her shirt as if ants had crawled down her bra.

"You might want to watch that," he said, balancing his own flake in the palm of one hand, à la pizza delivery boy. "If it gets down your shirt, you'll have to take that shirt off."

"Excuse me?" Her head popped up, pretty blue eyes wide.

"That's the only way you'll get it out of your clothes." He smiled, though he knew he should leave her alone. He just couldn't resist messing with her. "Once it's down your shirt, it'll keep poking at you all day."

"You're serious, aren't you?"

"Yup." He lifted a second wedge of hay he held while still balancing the first. "If you need a place to strip, you can do it right there." He winked. "I promise not to watch."

Her cheeks turned pink, her sexy mouth pressed together. It was exactly the reaction he'd been looking for. She didn't smile at him flirtatiously. Didn't seem to welcome his invitation to undress in front of him. Not, he quickly reassured himself, that he was looking for that. No, no. He'd just been curious. Obviously, she hadn't come to Texas to snare herself a cowboy bachelor.

Disappointed?

Absolutely not.

"The day I undress in front of you is the day the Tooth Fairy does the Macarena on your nose."

He found himself laughing despite himself.

"Maybe next time you'll listen to me," he said, heading off to feed.

"There won't be a next time," she shot back, and for some reason the words only made him smile all the more.

He kinda liked her spunk.

"STUPID, IMPOSSIBLE MAN," Jorie grumbled, listening for Ryan's footsteps outside as she quickly stripped out of her blouse. "'Next time maybe you'll listen to me,'" she mimicked, freezing for a moment when she heard a noise. It was just a horse snorting, though. Ryan was still busy feeding horses. She had no idea if he'd noticed her absence, and didn't care. He'd figure out what she was doing soon enough, she thought, shaking the silk fabric.

How in the heck was she going to adhere to Odelia's wishes to learn more about horses if she couldn't even feed them without messing it up?

Bits of green hay rained down like confetti. She had the stuff down her bra, too. Leaning forward, she scooped the cups out.

"Yuck."

A knock startled her.

"Go away," she called out.

He'd probably come to gloat. Evil man.

He knocked again. Louder.

"I said—"

The door opened.

"Hey!" She jerked her blouse in front of her.

"Are you okay?" Odelia asked, the woman's eyes filled with concern. "Ryan mentioned something about an accident."

The breath gushed out of her. "I thought you were Ryan."

"What happened?" Odelia slipped into the room, her eyes darting over Jorie quickly.

"I had hay down my shirt."

Odelia's face cleared, a hand lifting to her heart. "That's it? I thought it was serious."

"This *is* serious," Jorie quickly contradicted. "I feel

like I've rolled in a briar patch. I've got hay in places I didn't know I could have hay in."

The hand over her heart lifted to her mouth, Odelia's mirth clearly visible. "I can't believe that no-good piece of work otherwise known as my son actually let you feed."

"I insisted," Jorie admitted. "I know you want me to learn more about horses and so I thought this might be a simple introduction."

"It might have been if you hadn't been in your work clothes. Ridiculous man."

Jorie was ever so tempted to let Ryan take the fall. She really was. "Actually," she said, still holding the shirt in front of her. "He did warn me. Kind of."

"Come here," Odelia said, motioning with her finger for Jorie to approach.

Jorie didn't move.

Her new boss tipped her head at her in warning, hands moving to her hips. "Now, now, don't be modest," she drawled.

Jorie was completely bemused by the woman's own outfit. She wore a bright red Western shirt, one with beige piping across the front. There was no fringe today, but she had on the obligatory cowboy hat. Jeans encrusted with rhinestones completed the ensemble. It wouldn't be so bad, except she'd somehow managed to match the red of her shirt to the red of her lipstick. Not that it looked bad. It was just…unexpected on someone her age.

"Come on," she urged. "Give me your shirt. I've dealt with this problem before. You're not the first guest who's found themselves in this predicament."

Jorie handed over the shirt.

"I'll go outside and shake it out while you deal with

the other problem. And don't worry. I'll guard the door against that wretched son of mine."

But now that Odelia had arrived Jorie had to admit this was her own darn fault. If she hadn't been so stubborn this would never have happened.

Odelia returned quickly and Jorie felt better already, thanks to her de-hay-manation process, as she'd privately dubbed it. "If I never go near a brick of hay again, it'll be too soon," she muttered.

"They're called flakes, honey, and while I'm grateful that you took my words to heart, you really don't have to feed the horses."

Thank God for that.

"Come on," Odelia added. "Let me show you to the office you'll be sharing with my son."

Oh, yeah. The office. She'd forgotten.

Odelia swung the door wide, something brown dashing inside and causing her to step back until she realized it was a dog. The fluffy brown mutt yapped at her and Odelia shushed it, but it was no use. Another dog entered, this one equally small, only it was brown-and-white. Then a third dog entered. This one huge and shaggy. A black-and-white one followed, but it paused in the doorway, nose lifted as if trying to catch her scent.

"Whoa," Jorie said as the brown-and-white one jumped on her pants.

"Jackson, no," Odelia said.

Jackson didn't appear to hear very well. He kept bouncing up and down, the little brown one joining him now. The big brown dog shuffled up along side of her, thrust its head beneath her hand as if asking for a scratch. Out of the corner of her eye she caught the black-and-white dog, nose still lifted, nostrils quivering, its paws taking it ever closer to...

"My quiche," she cried, darting for the pie plate still atop a shelf.

"Your quiche?" Odelia echoed, only to repeat the words, "your quiche," and sounding horrified.

Jorie understood why a second later. With the accuracy of a laser-guided weapon, the dog darted.

"Brat, no!" Odelia lunged with a grace of someone in her twenties.

Brat—how appropriate, Jorie had time to think before she, too, made a mad dash for her breakfast.

Brat didn't appear to care that his name had been called. Nor that the word *no* had followed that name. Jorie watched as the pie plate slid into the dog's mouth with an ease that made her gasp.

"No," Odelia ordered.

The dog, pie plate hanging out of its mouth, glanced at the two humans charging toward him and did what any smart canine would do. He bolted for the door. Jorie tried to catch his collar, but she was nearly knocked off her feet by the big dog who'd suddenly caught the scent of his buddy's treasure. The two little dogs darted between her legs and Jorie almost fell to the ground. Odelia gave up the chase, turned, shot her a look of apology.

Jorie felt her shoulders slump. She'd really been looking forward to that quiche.

"Was someone looking for this?"

They both turned. Ryan stood by the door, pie plate in hand, although half the quiche was already gone. He smirked.

"Wretched dog," Odelia said.

When Jorie turned toward Odelia, the woman stared at her son, and it was clear she referred to her son, and not her miscreant canine.

Chapter Five

Ryan had to fight back laughter the whole way up the stairwell that led up to his office. He glanced back once, catching a glimpse of Jorie's downtrodden face. It wasn't funny, it really wasn't, but he'd been the victim of that wretched pack of dogs so many times that it sort of was...only not to Jorie.

He clutched the black iron stair rail that kept people from falling to the barn aisle below. Behind him he could hear his mother bringing up the rear, her red boots clopping on the wooden steps. When he glanced back one more time, two steps from the top of the landing, it was in time to catch his mother's glare...as if it was somehow his fault that her dogs had heisted Jorie's quiche.

"I have some oatmeal in my desk," he said, feeling guilty despite himself. He took the last step, pausing atop the parquet floor that made up the landing. The stairwell hugged the right side of the building, photos of some of their better-known ranch horses on the wall in between small, narrow windows that helped light the dark corner. "I can make you a quick bowl."

"That's okay," he heard Jorie say.

He stopped in front of two massive oak doors that guarded the entrance to his office like wooden drawbridges. Black iron hinges that matched the stairwell pointed toward the door handles.

"I'm sure I can find something later," she added.

He'd always thought the door was ostentatious, but his mom seemed to like it. Of course, the hinges squeaked horribly. He'd been meaning to fix that since forever. It didn't seem to bother his mom. She'd been the one to design the office space beyond.

"Don't you worry, dear," his mom said, joining the two of them on the landing, her hand finding Jorie's shoulder and patting it. "I've got plenty of food up at the house. I'll bring you something down just as soon as I get you settled into the office."

"If you bring her something, make sure you keep those dogs of yours locked up."

Yeah, that was definitely a glare coming from his mom, although what he'd done wrong he had no idea. He'd insisted the dogs be locked in the tack room while they showed Jorie her new workspace, but that'd been a matter of self-defense. The last time Mom's mutts had run amok in his office, they'd broken a lamp, ripped up a leather pillow and tried to eat a piece of furniture. The massive conference room table in the middle of the room beyond *still* bore Jackson's teeth marks.

"Our desks are on the left. Yours is the one on the right," Ryan told his mom's new employee as he inserted a key into the lock and swung the door wide.

He stepped aside, watching as Jorie's eyes widened when she caught sight of the office space beyond.

"Oh, wow."

The words weren't unexpected. Their guests frequently reacted that way—yes, even the seen-it-all oil executives that came to renegotiate oil rights every year. It'd taken his mom nearly a year to complete, having always considered herself something of an interior designer, and he had to admit, if there was one thing she was good at, it was making things look girlie. The office was like a cross between a Western saloon and a cattle baron's boudoir. Cowhide couches that could have sat an elephant to his left, the conference table in the middle of the room, made out of pine lodge poles and a massive glass tabletop that reminded Ryan of a miniature ice skating rink. To their left were three desks, all in a row, each of them facing out, toward the door. Above them, massive ceiling fans spun lazily through the air, their black iron hardware matching the other fixtures in the room.

"Do you like it?" his mom asked, sliding up next to Jorie so she could get a glimpse of Jorie's face. "My desk is right next to yours, and you're next to Ryan." She pointed toward his desk in the corner of the room. He had the most space, and a window. Actually, windows stretched across the front of the room, overlooking the parking area and the winding driveway that led to the ranch, pastures on both sides. "It took me forever to decorate, but I really think it works, don't you?"

Though his mom was nearly sixty years old, she could still sound like a little kid again. This was one of those moments. The room was striking, beautiful, but you could hear how badly she wanted Jorie's approval.

"Of course it looks great, Mom. You outdid yourself."

It was the tone of voice she used, that pleading little-girl-done-good question that hung in the air. He was a sucker for it every time.

So, apparently, was Jorie. "Oh, Mrs. Clayborne... are you kidding? This is stunning." To his surprise, although he had no idea why, the woman placed a comforting hand on his mother's shoulder. "It's truly beautiful. I love the view."

His mom beamed with pride. Oddly, it made his own heart swell, although not for the world would he let his mom see that. The last thing he needed was his mother realizing how much he wanted to please her. No way.

"Why thank you, Jorie. And, please, don't call me Mrs. Clayborne. It reminds me of Ryan's dad and how everyone called me Mrs. Clayborne this and Mrs. Clayborne that when he first brought me home. It was like I was Lady Bird Johnson for goodness' sake. Took me weeks to get used to it. I finally had to tell Mavis, our housekeeper, to stop."

She waved a hand in front of her face. Ryan marveled. She so rarely spoke about his dad anymore. It was like a scab she was afraid to itch for fear of making it bleed again. He knew exactly how she felt. He still missed his dad, too, though he'd died twenty years ago, when he was ten.

"Anyway," his mom was saying with a wave of her hand. "Come see the desk I picked out for you."

And by *picked,* his mom meant picked. It might look like the other two desks in the office, but there were subtle differences. It was blond oak like the other two which had been bought at the same time, but this one was more feminine. Not as thick-looking as the other two, which wasn't surprising since the mate to his desk had been bought for his dad back when the office had been behind the main house. *Excuse him.* The bridal suite now.

"It's handmade," said his mom. "A local craftsman made it just for you. Well, not you specifically, but for whoever I hired."

And it'd cost them a fortune. Not that they had to

worry about money, but that didn't mean Ryan liked spending a bundle on something that would have been just fine if it'd been made from pressed wood. He doubted anyone his mom hired would be around for long, especially since his mom probably wouldn't be planning weddings for very long.

"I've never seen anything so beautiful."

Ryan glanced at Jorie sharply, but she wasn't mouthing empty platitudes. She genuinely admired the desk, her pale hand drifting over the surface, Ryan wondering what it'd feel like to have that same hand—

Whoa.

He blinked, looked away, his gaze caught on his own desk. "Mom," he said. "I'm going to make Jorie a bowl of oatmeal. Why don't you show her where all the important things are?"

"You don't have to do that—"

But he was already moving off.

Putting some space between them.

What was it about the woman that made him want to ruffle her feathers? he thought, heading to the kitchenette in the left corner of the room. He wanted to tease her until she blushed, he admitted, grabbing a bowl from above the sink. He wasn't that way with Laurel. Yet he hardly knew this woman.

He glanced back, his mom waving her hand toward the conference table, Ryan hearing her mention the name of the famous craftsman who'd made it. He hardly paid attention as he poured oatmeal into a bowl, then some milk he didn't even remember grabbing from the mini-refrigerator below.

She was damn good-looking.

Yeah, so what? he asked himself, punching some buttons on the microwave. He'd seen plenty of good-looking women before. So what if she had thick, silky hair—the kind he liked best on a woman? And so what if her eyes were the same color as the forget-me-nots that grew wild in the pastures? Didn't mean a thing.

The microwave binged. Ryan grabbed the bowl, gasped and almost dropped it.

"Damn it."

He heard footsteps behind him. "Mmm. That smells good, doesn't it?" he heard his mom say. "Looks like it's not quite done, though. Stir it up a bit and put it on for another thirty seconds."

As if Ryan couldn't see that for himself.

"Why don't you sit down while I grab the file for the first wedding I want you to work on," he heard his mom say as he punched the buttons.

Ryan spun toward his mother.

"The Western wedding of the year."

"Mom—"

"Now, now, honey, don't be shy."

He wasn't being shy. He just didn't want Jorie to know he was about to get married.

And that was the scariest thought of all.

"Leave her be until after she eats breakfast," Jorie heard Ryan say.

The smell of oatmeal drove her crazy.

"Nonsense," his mom answered, hooking an arm into hers and guiding her to a chair.

She was so grateful for that chair.

There had been times during her office tour when she thought she might pass out, but it was her own stupid fault, she thought, all but collapsing into the seat. If she hadn't been so hardheaded and determined to prove to Odelia's son that she was here to work, not sleep, she might have been in her new house, unpacking, maybe even still sleeping…and definitely eating. Yes, absolutely, positively, for sure eating.

Her stomach yelled at her impatiently.

Instead she found herself sitting at a table as big as a bocce ball court hoping against hope that the same son she was determined to impress would bring her a damn bowl of oatmeal. And soon.

"I can't wait to hear your ideas," Odelia was saying.

"Mom—" her son said again, louder this time, as if the sound of the microwave might be drowning out his words.

Hurry up, oatmeal.

"Ryan's been so quiet about it all, and his fiancée is so sweet she won't say a word. She prefers to leave everything up to me instead. Says I'm the pro, but we all know I'm hardly that…"

Jorie blinked.

Fiancée?

"…*you're* the expert," Odelia was saying, "which is why I'm turning the whole thing over to *you*."

Engaged.

"Mom, she hasn't even had breakfast. Give her a moment, will you?"

Get it together, Jorie. It's no big deal. So he's engaged. What was so surprising about that?

Funny, he never mentioned it.

"When's the wedding?" she heard herself ask.

But why would *he mention it?*

Odelia's brow wrinkled beneath her hat. "That's the kicker."

Jorie's heart began to race like the minute hand of a watch.

"I know it's a lot to ask," Odelia said, "especially since you just started…"

"Mom, really. She doesn't have to work on my wedding."

"End of next month," Odelia blurted.

Six weeks? Was she kidding?

"I know that doesn't give you a whole lot of time. If it's any consolation, the kids just told me about it last week, but we can do it. We've already got the location. All we need are a few minor details ironed out."

"Here." A bowl of oatmeal was set in front of her, its steam wafting up and teasing her nose. She watched Ryan's eyes dart over her face. They were filling with something like concern. Concern and something else, something she couldn't quite put her finger on. "I put some brown sugar and milk on it. Hope that's okay."

Gone was the teasing smile. In its place was a look that appeared almost troubled.

Engaged.

Of course. He was a hardworking, attractive male who would one day inherit a huge ranch. Frankly, she was surprised someone hadn't snapped him up years ago. Half the eligible females in the county must have set their caps at him over the years.

"Eat," Odelia ordered, the woman's kindly blue-green eyes filled with encouragement.

She felt rather than saw Ryan move back from the table. He hovered near her for a moment, almost as if he was waiting to see how she liked the oatmeal. The spoon she picked up felt cold in her hands. She took a bite and almost sighed in delight as the hot food filled her mouth.

"I'm going down to the maintenance barn. Gonna

lay materials out for Sam," she heard Ryan say. "So we can get started on replacing those boards."

"Oh, perfect," Odelia said. "Jorie can see where you're going to get married."

The spoon froze halfway between the bowl and her mouth, and though she'd only had a few mouthfuls, it didn't taste as good as it had a moment before.

"She can do that tomorrow."

When she met Ryan's gaze, his concern for the way she was looking—because that's what it'd been, she suddenly realized—had faded. He didn't look happy. Odelia, however, appeared oblivious to his discontent.

"Hurry up and eat that oatmeal, dear," she said. "Ryan's going to give you a tour of the ranch."

And for some strange reason, Jorie lost her appetite.

Chapter Six

She looked about as happy to be with him as he felt, Ryan thought, walking her toward the all-terrain vehicle that looked like a kid's toy. It was a miniaturized truck, right down to the bed in the back and the enclosed cab in the front. Its bright green color nearly perfectly matched the grassy backdrop. Though the sun was higher now, it was still early morning, the grass a deep green.

"We're not allowed to drive regular-sized vehicles down to the barn," he said, hoping to break the ice by injecting a note of humor. "God forbid we gouge tracks into the virgin soil."

"How long have you known your fiancée?"

"All my life."

And he had. Laurel was like a sister, someone who always seemed to be underfoot…which seemed like an odd way to think of his fiancée, he admitted to himself. But she was his best friend, which was why he'd agreed—

He didn't want to think about that.

She was nodding as she slid inside the golf-cart-sized cab. She still wore the same outfit, and even though her slacks were supposed to conceal the shape of her legs he could still imagine the tanned length of them beneath the black fabric.

Stop it.

He slammed the door closed with more force than necessary. Accident. That's all it was. His hand found the crown of his Stetson and lifted it, his free hand scratching his forehead before cramming the hat back down on his head.

He was just a man in need of a little hanky-panky. Lord knows he wouldn't get that from Laurel. Not now. Maybe not ever.

That's the life you're signing up for, bud. Better get used to it.

He rounded the vehicle to the driver's side and reached for the door handle, causing his nails to bend back, a bolt of pain shooting up his fingers and into his arm. He jumped back and shook his hand to ease the stinging. "Son of a—"

"You okay?" he heard her ask.

No, he wanted to gasp. He was far from okay. Ever since she'd arrived he'd been on edge. Short-tempered. Maybe even rude. Ah, hell. All he knew was that he didn't want to drive Miss Daisy around the ranch when what he really needed to do was get to work.

He tried the door again. Thankfully it opened smoothly this time.

"Let's go." And even to his own ears, his voice sounded harsh.

"Good thing you don't have false nails."

He glanced over at her.

"It's a form of torture when you bend them back if you have acrylic nails on."

The sun, which had climbed higher, caught the edge of her hair, setting it aglow.

"Hurts for hours," she added.

"I'll take your word for it."

Okay. Fine. So he couldn't get the image of her on that bed out of his mind. So what?

He started the engine, grabbed the gear shift on the dash and slammed it into gear. The vehicle lurched. They both about clocked their heads.

"Are you okay?" he asked, his hand shooting out of its own volition and landing on her leg. It felt like touching an open wire. "Sorry."

Holy crap. What was that?

He glanced over at her. She'd felt it, too. He could tell by the way she was looking to the left and then straight ahead and then right again—anywhere but at him.

She coughed. Cleared her throat. "So tell me about her."

He didn't want to talk about Laurel. He wanted to figure out why touching her made his whole body twitch with…something. Laurel was none of her business.

Only it was.

It was bad enough his mom had hired a helper. All right, a damn sexy-looking "assistant" as it turned out, but now that that woman was supposed to plan his wedding…

This wasn't going to be easy. Of course, he'd known that. The plain and simple truth was that he didn't love Laurel, his fiancée. How the hell was he going to explain *that?* Laurel's pregnancy was a secret only the two of them shared. Well, that complete jerk-off of a man she'd been involved with knew, but he'd run off. Laurel flatly refused to abort the pregnancy, and he didn't blame her. The problem was Laurel's dad. As old-fashioned as they come, Lyle Harrington would lose his mind if he found out his only child was pregnant, and that the jerk he'd specifically warned Laurel against dating, Thad Norton, had run out on her. So two weeks ago, while Laurel was crying in his arms over the whole darn thing, he'd come up with a scheme. *He'd* marry her. Temporarily, of course, because he didn't relish the thought of being hitched to a woman he didn't love. He could do it temporarily, at least until the dust settled, *that* he didn't mind, and yet suddenly what had seemed like a good idea two weeks ago felt like a really *bad* idea now. A really, *really* bad idea.

He glanced at Jorie's legs again.

"Laurel is…" he searched for a word "…loyal."

Crap. What kind of answer was that? Loyal. He made his fiancée sound like a damn dog.

"Loyal, huh?" he heard her ask, a touch of amusement in her voice.

He refused to look at her again, had to keep his eyes firmly straight ahead, hands locked on the steering wheel, jaw thrust forward to the point that it hurt.

Relax.

Yeah, right. Taking her out to look at the wedding venue was the first item on a long list of prewedding tasks that he'd have to muddle through, for Laurel's sake. He just wished he didn't feel like such a fraud.

"I've known Laurel my entire life," he said, feeling Jorie's gaze on him. He could picture her blue eyes perfectly. They were the blue of a peacock feather—iridescent, striking, mesmerizing. Funny, he couldn't recall the exact color of Laurel's eyes at all.

"So were you high school sweethearts?"

Ryan's fingernails dug into the foam that covered the steering wheel. "Something like that."

She didn't need to know the details. All he had to do was deliver her to the barn, maybe leave her there. She could walk back to the office, he thought, pointing the vehicle toward the top of a small hill.

Okay, so that might not be the polite thing to do, but he felt as jumpy as a flea in a vet's office.

"Oh, wow," he heard her gasp.

He'd crested the top of the hill where the view was one he'd seen at least a thousand times before, and yet for some reason this morning he saw it through new eyes.

"It really is something, isn't it?"

The sun, still low on the horizon, painted the barn orange and pink and deep red. The metal roof had a patina that blended seamlessly with the colors; it added to the warmth of the picture. The colors of fall, he thought, suddenly hankering for pumpkin pie and apple cider.

"You're very lucky to live here."

The longing in her voice caused him to turn his head and stare at her profile. He slowed down before he could think better of it, and as they coasted to a stop a few hundred feet away, he'd have been blind not to spot the sadness in her gaze.

"I've never known any other place," he replied.

They came to a stop. Her blue gaze met his own. No. Not sadness…pain.

"Every kid should grow up in a place like this."

He knew then that she had not, that memories of her childhood were painful, and that as a youth she had longed for wide-open spaces and an old barn to play in.

And apparently, you've developed psychic abilities in the past half hour.

He scoffed at himself, pressed the accelerator again. "Come on. I'll show you the inside."

IT WAS JUST an empty barn.

Four-inch-wide timbers threw back the sound of Jo-

rie's heels as she walked into the middle of the cavern-
ous space.

"This used to house my great-great-grandfather's
cows."

She refused to look him in the eye, still felt the rem-
nants of…whatever it was she'd felt back in his ATV.

"It's much bigger on the inside than I thought it
would be." And there would be ways to improve it.
Already her mind was spinning, which was good, because the last thing she wanted to think about was Ryan
Clayborne and the strange fission of energy that had
danced between them earlier. The ceilings were high,
so much so that she wondered if there hadn't been an
attic ages ago.

"Did there used to be a hayloft here?"

"Yes. When we renovated the barn for weddings we
took it out. Mom wanted high ceilings for the ambience." He stressed the word *ambience,* doing his best
to imitate his mom's voice and failing.

"I like it," she said.

Her voice echoed off the concrete floor, her gaze
hooking on the gray aggregate. That would need to be
changed, too. Maybe some brown stain on the floor,
something that would blend in better. And maybe a
chandelier. That might seem strange, but she would bet
it would look good. Nothing fancy, just something that
could be decorated with flowers or jewels or whatever
a bride might like.

"Any chance we could add some more windows?"
It wasn't superdark inside, but it was bad enough. The
place resembled a mortuary more than a wedding chapel. "More natural light would really brighten things
up."

She heard his "Hmm" as he contemplated her question. "I don't see why not. 'Course, you'd have to clear it with my mom."

"Is there power?"

She finally gained the courage to look him in the eye again only to immediately wish she hadn't. Every time her gaze ensnared his own, something tickled her stomach, a something that made her skin sprout goose bumps and made her think she'd lost her mind, a something that had multiplied tenfold when he'd touched her earlier.

Hello. You're here to check out this place for this man's wedding.

"No. We bring in generators if we need light."

That must really add to the ambience. She almost said the words out loud, making a mental note to tell Odelia the sound of generators humming in the background was *not* romantic.

"Okay, I've seen enough."

She heard the footfalls of his boots on concrete as he fell into step behind her. She really didn't like the man. He was cocky and so full of himself she found herself wanting to get under his skin because…because…well, just because.

"We've got some work ahead of us," she said after slipping inside his mini truck vehicle, whatever it was called.

It felt as though she sat next to an elephant. That's how aware she was of him, and it was ridiculous, too. How could you not like someone and yet be aware of him? Aware, aware. As in exquisitely conscious of his dark good looks. Of how his eyes brought to mind warm seas and fields of bluebonnets. Of how razor stubble already sprouted upon his chin, and how she wanted to see if it felt like sandpaper if she rubbed it. He smelled. That was the worst part. She kept catching the same whiff of masculine essence that she'd noticed yesterday and it made her want to scream in anger, not at him, but at her. He was her boss's son. And engaged. She had no business having lusty thoughts about him, yet she'd had exactly that. Last night. Just before he'd awoken her in bed. His legs had been entangled with her own—at least in her dream—because when she'd opened her eyes, it'd been the sheets, not—

She cut the thought off.

"Do you know how much your mom is willing to spend on upgrades?"

"You'll have to discuss that with her."

His voice sounded gruff, as if he were angry about something. Maybe he didn't like to discuss money.

"I'll work up a list of things I'd like to see done to the barn before your wedding."

There. She'd said it. *His* wedding.

"Like what?" he asked.

Though she'd just met him, she found herself feeling something that seemed an awful lot like disappointment that he was engaged.

Ridiculous.

"I'd like to stain the floor. Make it more natural. And I bet you're using folding chairs for services. I'd like to get some old pews."

"Pews?"

"You know, the kind in churches. They sell them off from time to time. You just have to keep your eyes out. It'd make it look more romantic—"

"It's a barn, not a damn wedding hall."

He sounded so annoyed she found herself glancing at him in surprise. He'd thrust his jaw forward, his hands gripping the steering wheel more tightly than he needed. She could see the white of his knuckles.

"If you're worried about the expense, you can relax. It'll cost next to nothing to do what I want to do."

He glanced over at her, something that was a cross between amusement and annoyance on his face. "Believe me, the last thing we need to worry about is money."

Yeah, that didn't surprise her. The house and property certainly suggested they were rich, but she'd learned over the years that looks could be deceiving, which is why she'd formed the opinion that maybe holding weddings on their property was a way to generate extra revenue.

Apparently that wasn't the case at all.

"I just don't want to see this turn into a three-ring circus." His words came out quickly, as if he were confessing something to a priest.

She exhaled, having not even realized she was holding her breath. "By 'this' you mean your wedding?"

He nodded.

"I see."

He slowed down. They were at the top of the small hill, the one that overlooked the main portion of the ranch. In the distance she could see his mother's home, the covered arena where their office was and the various outbuildings. The grass beneath their vehicle seemed to breathe deeply and warm, moisture-laden air clung to her skin. She was used to Georgia's humidity, but Texas humidity felt different. Hotter. Warmer. Thicker.

"I want to keep this simple," he said, causing her to look over at him again. "So does my—" she watched his Adam's apple bob "—my bride."

"I take it you're the kind of groom that wants to keep his distance from the wedding plans?"

"Something like that."

"All right then," she said, injecting as much enthusiasm as she could muster into the words. "I'll keep you out of it, but I'm going to need to talk to your bride. What's her name again?"

"Laurel."

"Is there a way to get in touch with Laurel?"

"My mom will give you that information."

His mother? Couldn't he just rattle off a cell phone number? Not that she had anything to write with, but still.

"Will she be around today?"

He wouldn't look at her. She followed his gaze. As far as the eye could see, there was grassland, so perfectly cropped it looked as if a bolt of multicolored green fabric had been rolled out upon the earth. In the distance, maybe a few miles out, the trees thickened up, a darker color that added texture to the scene. It was so perfectly beautiful Jorie found herself thinking no artist on earth could ever capture the essence of the place.

How wonderful to grow up here.

"I'll have Laurel stop by the office."

The vehicle lurched. Jorie found herself reaching for something to hold on to. As they drove around the ranch, Ryan showing her the creek in the distance, and then explaining which pastures held cows, and which held the horses, and which held the weanlings, whatever that was, she began to think she'd missed something back there, something important, something directly related to Ryan's wedding.

A wedding he didn't want to be involved in.

That wasn't so strange. Sometimes a groom wanted nothing to do with a wedding. Yet Ryan didn't strike her as the type. From what she'd seen in the past twenty-four hours, he was involved in every aspect of the ranch, but not this.

The question was, why?

Chapter Seven

It wasn't until Monday that Jorie finally met Ryan's bride, though she was in the office for nearly half the day before she heard someone pull up outside of the arena. A quick glance revealed a brown-haired woman that Jorie was almost certain had to be Laurel. She waited, kept glancing toward the door. She'd spent the weekend observing two of the weddings Odelia had scheduled, taking notes. Actually, she'd worked throughout the entire weekend, half expecting to run into Ryan at some point. She hadn't. This morning she'd heard his truck, had looked out the window and observed him driving away beneath an overcast and gloomy-looking sky, and immediately felt the urge to climb back under the sheets and cover her head.

"Hello?"

The word came from the other side of the door. Young and innocent sounding, and since the only person she was half expecting was...

"Laurel?" Jorie called, pasting a smile on her face as she went to the door, although why the woman didn't just come right on inside, Jorie had no idea.

"Oh!" said a tiny brunette with the prettiest gray eyes she'd ever seen. The loud squeak of the door's hinges reminded Jorie of a castle's jail cell, although maybe that was just her own twisted imagination. "I didn't expect the door to open like that."

"You must be Laurel."

The woman smiled, and Jorie admitted she wasn't at all what she expected. For some reason she'd pictured a voluptuous blonde. Or maybe someone sleek and elegant with designer jeans and a two-thousand-dollar cowboy hat—if they made cowboy hats that expensive. The diminutive-looking brunette had a grin that wrinkled the corners of her eyes and lit up her face.

"And you must be Jorie." She held out her hand, her grip as soft as her eyes.

"Come on in." Jorie stepped back from the door. "My desk is over here." She glanced behind the woman, thinking that Ryan might be with her. He wasn't, of course, which would explain why Laurel had knocked.

"I'm so nervous," Laurel said as she took a seat. She wore her hair long and loose, her white T-shirt and plain-Jane jeans so completely casual Jorie wasn't certain what to think. Was she making a statement? "I was actually sort of hoping Ryan's mother would be here."

"She had some errands to run." Although Jorie wondered if Ryan's mother had even been told Laurel was stopping by. Something told Jorie she hadn't.

"Oh, that's too bad." Laurel clasped her hands in her lap, looking around her. She appeared curious about her surroundings, her head turning left and right, long hair flicking this way and that. "I've only been in here a few times."

"Really?" And she was engaged to Ryan? Jorie opened a desk drawer to her right. She'd spent a good portion of her weekend getting herself organized. To that end, she pulled out a manila folder with "Clayborne-Harrington Wedding" handwritten on the tab.

"I would have thought you'd have been up here tons of times."

The quick shake of her head brought to mind a young girl. She even smelled like one. Jorie tried to place the scent. Ivory soap. Jorie would bet on it.

"No," she drawled in her Texas twang, pretty gray eyes meeting her own again. "Ryan keeps to himself when he's working. Why, I hardly ever see him."

That must be why their relationship worked.

"I'm thinking you'll be seeing a lot of this office in the coming weeks."

The woman looked away for a moment. "Yes, I will."

What was with these two? They both acted as if they were planning a funeral, not a wedding.

"Let's go over what I've got so far." Jorie opened up the folder. "We've got the barn booked for the last week in October. That means maybe a fall theme."

Blank stare.

"Or maybe a *Twilight* sort of theme?"

Blank stare.

"You know, a bit of a Gothic vampire look."

She was kidding, but the woman took her seriously, shaking her head again, like a dog trying to get water out of its ears. "I don't think that would work."

"No," Jorie muttered, "probably not."

"I think we're looking at more of a traditional wedding."

"Traditional. Got it. Big veil, poufy wedding dress, the man you love holding your hand."

Laurel's eyes got big. They turned red. Then they filled with tears. "Yeah," she said, quickly looking away. "Something like that."

Okay, what the heck was going on? Had Laurel and

Ryan gotten into a fight? Was that why she hadn't seen him this morning?

"Maybe we should do this another time?"

"No, no," Laurel said. "I'm all right. It's just, I'm just—"

And Jorie found herself holding her breath.

What?

Laurel couldn't stand her fiancé anymore and so she wanted to call off the wedding? She'd changed her views on marriage? She'd met another man?

"Everything's happened so fast. I'm just feeling a little overwhelmed."

And why are you so disappointed by the answer, Ms. Jorie?

"That happens," Jorie said, scooting her chair around her desk and reaching for the woman's hand. "Just take deep breaths. I promise, this won't be so bad. We've got the venue booked. That's usually half the battle. Odelia has a list of local caterers and wedding cake designers and entertainment. All you have to do is pick things out. Speaking of that, have you bought a dress?"

"No."

Oookay, another hurdle to overcome, and quite frankly, rather strange. The woman had been engaged for at least a couple weeks, and she hadn't gone wedding dress shopping? That was usually the first thing women did once the engagement ring was on the finger. Speaking of that, Laurel didn't sport a twinkling token of Ryan's love. Not even a promise of that love, as in a promise ring.

Jorie's radar pinged again.

"When do you plan to go shopping?"

"Soon." There was no happy smile. No wiggle of excitement. Not even a giddy sigh of delight.

"Did you need some help?"

"No, no," Laurel said. "I can do it on my own."

Okay, so she didn't have a dress. Didn't have a ring. And she didn't have a clue.

Houston, we have a problem.

"I'll tell you what. I'll line up some appointments with local boutiques. I'll also come up with a game plan for your wedding. A sort of jumping-off point. You can tell me if you like what I've come up with, or not. If you don't like it, we'll start over again." Jorie snapped her fingers. "Easy as pie."

"Oh, thank you," Laurel gushed.

"It's my job." She gave the woman a chipper smile. "My pleasure." She closed the Clayborne-Harrington file. "Give me a couple of days for some of this, but come by the office tomorrow for the list of wedding boutiques. That's going to be your top priority this week—finding a dress."

The woman nodded, slowly stood. "Thank you so much."

Jorie stood, too, and no sooner had she rounded the corner of her desk than the door opened again.

"Did I miss the big planning session?"

Laurel turned. "Daddy!"

A tall, gangly-looking man had entered, one who seemed to have aged before his time. He wore a black cowboy hat along with his jeans and blue-checkered shirt, and he had eyes as bright as the lights of New York when he stared at his daughter.

"I hope I'm not too late," he said.

He was also carrying something, Jorie noticed, something made of tulle that nearly dragged along the ground. A veil.

"We were just finishing up, Mr. Harrington." Jorie

held out her hand. "And it looks like you have something for Laurel."

Okay, he wasn't just tall. He was *tall*. Jorie had to crane her neck back to look up at him.

"How did you sneak up on us so quietly?" Laurel slipped into her dad's arms, a wide smile on her face. The veil swirled around Laurel's back, but she didn't notice. Her eyes closed when she hugged her dad.

The twinges of envy Jorie felt had her looking away.

"I swear I didn't even hear you come up the steps."

Mr. Harrington smiled. "I parked around the side." He stepped back and held out the veil. "I wanted to surprise you with this."

The veil swirled once again. Like a wisp of early morning fog, it hung there, Laurel's eyes filling with tears as she eyed it up and down.

"You found it," she said softly.

"I knew where it was all the time."

Laurel took the veil gently, reverently. "It's so beautiful."

And it was. Jorie had seen a lot of veils, but this one had tiny flowers stitched around the edge—and she would bet those rosebuds were hand-sewn, too.

"I love it," Laurel said, spinning around as if looking for a mirror.

"In the bathroom," Jorie gently prompted.

Laurel tore off. Jorie turned to her father. "You must be very proud."

The man's light blue eyes found her own. "She's so much like her mother it makes my heart swell."

And there were tears in his eyes, too. Jorie swallowed, wondering what it would have been like to grow up like Laurel did. To know you were loved. Forever. No questions asked.

"How's it look?" Jorie called over the lump in her throat.

"I love it."

Jorie moved forward then.

Get a grip.

No big deal. If Laurel saw her tears, she'd attribute them to the beauty of the moment.

"Isn't it stunning?" Laurel asked as Jorie slid up behind her. She was holding it above the top of her head, and Jorie noticed it had a jeweled crown. Nothing too ornate, but fancy enough that it sparkled even in the bathroom's low light.

"It's beautiful, Laurel. We'll have to see if we can find a dress to match."

Something about her words caused Laurel's eyes to dim. "Yes. The wedding."

"To Ryan," Jorie felt she should add, though why she said that, she had no idea.

"My wedding to Ryan."

It was as though someone had switched the bathroom lights off. Laurel's hand lowered. She scooped up the veil in her arms so it wouldn't drag and pasted a bright smile on her face just before she turned.

"I love it, Daddy. Thank you."

"You're welcome, honey."

The two hugged again.

"Where's that fiancé of yours, by the way?"

Laurel slipped from her father's arms once again. "I told you. He has to work."

The man glanced around as if expecting Ryan to suddenly appear. "Well, I guess I can't hardly blame him. Weddings are for women to plan." He clasped his daughter's upper arms. "I can't tell you how proud I am of you, too. After all these years, to finally realize it was Ryan you loved." The man covered his chest with his fist. "I couldn't be happier for you, honey."

Jorie hung back, watching. There was something in Laurel's eyes, something that made Jorie's radar ping again.

"Thank you, Daddy." She looked away quickly.

"Come on. I'll walk you to your car."

It was like watching an actress get in character. Laurel opened her eyes, turned and smiled. She squeezed her dad's arm before looking at Jorie, and then, before Jorie knew what she was about, enveloped Jorie in a hug, the tulle from the veil hitting her in the face.

"I can't tell you how much I appreciate all your help."

Jorie found herself patting the woman's back awkwardly. "That's okay."

"I mean it, Jorie." She leaned back, clutched Jorie's upper arms, the veil dancing through the air once again. "I can already tell you're a lifesaver."

As she stared into Laurel's sweet gray eyes, Jorie saw need there. And maybe even a twinge of desperation. And sadness.

What did she have to be sad about?

"Thank you," Laurel said.

Maybe she was overwhelmed. Maybe she was the type of bride that panicked under pressure, that was so stressed by the whole ordeal it made her scared. And maybe that was a better way to describe what Jorie saw in her eyes.

"Tell Ryan I'll see him later." She smiled up at Jorie and stepped away.

"I'll do that."

But as she watched the woman head to the door, she couldn't help but think there was more to Ryan and Laurel's story than met the eye. She couldn't quite put her finger on what it was, but something was off. She hadn't been in the business for ten years without learning a thing or two.

RYAN STARED AT the stairwell as if he contemplated climbing Mt. Everest.

Go on. She's not going to bite.

"Damn it." He patted a spot of dirt on his jeans as if worried about his appearance, which he was not, idly watching the puffs of dust that filled the air.

He'd lost his privacy, he thought, taking the first step. Sure, he'd shared the office with his mom in the past, but this was different. His mom was gone half the time. Now he was forced to share it with a woman who'd been on his mind since her arrival. All morning long he'd wondered how her meeting with Laurel had gone. Did she suspect the two of them weren't in love? Had Laurel given the game away?

He'd reached the top of steps he couldn't even remember climbing, found himself pausing outside the door and listening for sounds on the other side. Maybe she wasn't in there. Maybe she'd left for lunch or something.

If only he were that lucky.

The moment he opened the door he spotted her, sitting at her desk, peeking up at him when she heard the hinges creak.

"I guess I need to get off my butt and oil those." He pointed to the *V*-shaped steel.

"Please do," she said with a tiny smile. "It's driving me nuts."

It hit him then. He wanted Jorie. He'd been instantly attracted to her from the moment she'd stepped out of her car. It hadn't helped to see her half-naked. Something about her laying there, about the way she'd looked all wrapped up in the sheet, had him thinking thoughts he had no business thinking, especially given the fact she was planning his wedding.

His wedding.

He took his hat off, rubbing his hands through his hair before hanging the hat by the door. He almost hated to face her. She wore a fluffy off-white sweater, something that hugged her shoulders and neck and highlighted her smooth, pale complexion.

"I was beginning to think you weren't coming in today."

He took a deep breath, found himself squaring his own shoulders like a boxer about to take to the ring.

"I had some catching up to do."

His voice came out sounding gruff, but he told himself that was for the better. He didn't need her getting ideas.

Yeah, it wouldn't look good if she spotted the way his damn cheeks turned red at just the thought of sitting next to her. He'd turned into a damn thirteen-year-old boy over the weekend.

"I met your bride today."

He nearly winced, caught himself just in time, and managed to croak out, "Oh, yeah?"

"And her father."

"Oh?" Lyle had been here? Thank God he'd missed that. He was finding it harder and harder to look the man in the eyes.

"He brought Laurel a present. A wedding veil that I take it her mother wore."

A wedding veil. For their wedding. Crap, all of this was becoming more and more real.

Well, of course it's real. You're marrying the girl.

"She seems…sweet."

He caught the pause, found himself meeting her gaze despite the sickness in his stomach. She'd put her hair atop her head, some kind of poufy hairstyle with curly tendrils escaping from the back. It made her cheekbones look high and sexy.

Sexy?

Yeah, like a lingerie model.

"I take it you were expecting overbearing and ostentatious."

To his surprise, she appeared to consider the question, her head tipping to the side. Pearl earrings, the long and dangling type, swung from her ears. What would those ears taste like?

"I don't know what I was expecting," she admitted, her pretty blue eyes narrowing for a moment. "But she's really nice. So is her dad."

Everyone loved Laurel, including the man who'd gotten her pregnant—or so he'd claimed. He'd run out on her the moment he'd discovered she was pregnant. Apparently, responsibility was all it'd taken for the man to fall *out* of love. And now Ryan was forced to pick up the pieces.

"She's a good girl."

Something sparked in Jorie's gaze, something that made him instantly regret his words. Damn it. She was too smart. He realized that was part of his attraction.

"She didn't have a whole lot to say about the wedding."

No. Of course not. Laurel was too distraught over the whole Thad thing to plan their wedding.

The noose of commitment began to tighten around his neck. Sure, offering to marry Laurel had seemed like the right thing to do, but that didn't make the decision any less hard to live with. He wasn't in love with his future wife. He'd never love her, except as a friend, and had looked upon their marriage as a temporary thing. But it was much more than that, he suddenly realized. Despite not loving Laurel, he would never be unfaithful. He refused to take a chance that someone might find out, might hurt Laurel even though she was no more in love with him than Ryan was with her. Still, he owed her his fidelity, no matter what a sham their relationship might be.

"She's that way," Ryan found himself saying. "Not very assertive. You'll need to guide her a bit."

Her look seemed to say, "A bit?"

"She's been very sheltered her whole life."

So much so that pregnancy outside of marriage had been a calamity. She'd come to him sobbing, so distraught over the whole situation that she'd damn near made herself sick.

"Just be patient," he said.

But the advice was more to himself than to Jorie. Of course, she didn't know that.

"I've set up appointments for her to visit some of the local boutiques. Does she have any friends that she could go shopping with?"

Did she? Ryan was abashed to admit he didn't know. "I believe she does," he hedged. "I'll make sure she goes."

Another one of Jorie's looks, the kind that reminded Ryan of one of his mom's dogs. Curious. As if she were listening to words she didn't understand, head tilted to the side.

"Maybe I should go with her."

That thought had him feeling sick all over again. "No. Don't do that. I'll send her out with someone."

"What about her mother?"

"Doesn't have one." He busied himself fussing with his files, though they were all in perfect order and what he needed to do was check feed lot bills against invoices. "Her mom died when she was ten."

"Oh. That's horrible."

That was why she'd been coddled by her father. Ryan had long thought that Lyle Harrington feared to lose his daughter like he had his wife in a car wreck years ago.

"My mom stepped in and became a surrogate mother to her."

Funny, he'd never thought of it that way, yet that's exactly what happened. That's why Laurel felt more like a little sister than a fiancée.

"So, why doesn't your mom go shopping with her?"

His stomach turned.

"She's too busy. We have another wedding this weekend, and then there's the cutting competition she's trying to get ready for, and some charity thing she's helping with."

"Cutting?"

Ryan nodded. "It's where a horse works with cattle. My mom has to pull a steer out of a herd and then keep it away from the other steers. You'd probably enjoy watching."

"I'll take your word for it. Right now I'm feeling a little overwhelmed. Not," she quickly reassured, "that that's a bad thing. I like being busy. It's just that your mom wants me to focus this week on getting to know the local vendors and coming up with ideas for any holiday weddings we might book for next year. That's my main focus right now, marketing Christmas weddings and selling our services to future brides."

Oh, great.

"But I honestly think your mother would love to go shopping with Laurel."

"No."

There it was again, that something he saw in her eyes, the something that made him think she was on to him.

"What about a ring?" she asked. "When were you planning on getter her that?"

So she spotted that, huh? Great. He scratched at his forehead, trying to think of what to say. "I'm working on it," was the best he could come up with.

Her thick lashes lowered, eyes glittering. "You're working on it?"

Geez, she reminded him of his mother. "Laurel doesn't seem to mind."

"Get her a ring."

He heard the door open behind him and groaned.

Just as he feared, behind him came the words, "You haven't gotten her a ring?"

Terrific. His *mother*.

Chapter Eight

How did she sneak up on them? Jorie wondered. That was twice today someone had done that. Worse, she spotted one of Odelia's little doggie friends right at her heels. It was the long-haired brown one. Jorie quickly scanned her desk for food. Nothing left for the little thief to steal, thank goodness.

"Mom," her son warned. "We said no dogs up here."

"That's right. No *dogs,* honey," his mom said. "Plural. There's nothing wrong with having my little Herbie up here. Now, what's this about no ring?"

Her little Herbie made a beeline for Jorie's lap, much to Odelia's obvious delight. Jorie froze.

"That's why we call him that," she said. "He's a lovebug."

Her lovebug had dog breath, Jorie thought, trying not to breathe too deeply.

"Ryan?" Odelia said in a tone of voice Jorie remembered from her own, troubled childhood.

"Okay, fine. No. I haven't gotten Laurel a ring. I was kind of thinking you might have one you could give me to use."

Kind of thinking? What was this? Didn't he want to pick out that ring?

"Good heavens, Ryan, I thought Laurel wasn't wear-

ing a ring because you were having it sized or something."

Jorie wondered if Odelia knew the half of it.

"I was going to get around to it."

His mother turned one of the conference table chairs
around and seemed to wilt into it. "Ryan, I could cheer-
fully kill you. No wonder Laurel's been moping around
here lately. She probably thinks you don't love her."

And there it was again, the splash of color that
crept up from his jawline and spilled into his cheeks.
It matched the color of his shirt, a soft red that reminded
Jorie of cranberries. He looked like a painted cherub
with those blotches of red.

"I've been busy."

"Too busy to buy your bride an engagement ring?"

Jorie came to his rescue. "Is there a local jeweler
in town?"

"Yes, there's about a half dozen," Odelia answered.
"I have something he can use, too. You're welcome to
it, Ryan. Belonged to your great-grandmother, but it'll
need to be sized. My hands are huge compared to Laurel's." Odelia's lips pressed together, clearly perturbed.
"Do you even know what size she is?"

No answer.

"I'll find out," Jorie said. "In fact, I'll set up an ap-
pointment with the jeweler. That way Ryan can either
drop your ring off for sizing or pick something out."

"Pick something out."

He shot the words out so quickly Jorie found herself
turning toward him in surprise. His blush had faded. He
now leaned back in his chair, arms crossed.

"She'll want something new," he added.

Frankly, Laurel struck her as a traditional type,

someone who would cherish a family heirloom—like the veil.

"Fine," his mom said. "Jorie will go with you to pick something out. You don't mind, do you, Jorie?"

Jorie resisted the urge to groan. "I was hoping to catch up on some paperwork."

"You can do that later," Odelia said. "I've been wanting you to meet all the local vendors face to face. You can do that after helping Ryan."

Jorie's face felt as if it would crack. "Uh, sure." She gave Odelia a can-do smile.

Odelia wasn't even paying attention to her. She was staring at her son, a frown on her face.

"There's a list of jewelers on the contact list I gave you. Call Richard's, they're the best. Ryan will drive you."

She jerked so harshly she almost dumped Herbie off her lap. "Sorry," she said, patting the dog on the head absently, perhaps even a bit too hard. "That's not necessary. I'm sure he's busy." She smiled at Ryan politely. "I can meet you there around three."

"You'll go now," Odelia ordered.

Now?

Herbie jumped off her lap at nearly the exact moment that Odelia stood up.

"Mom, I'm sure Jorie's busy—"

"*Now,* Ryan." Her tone was so harsh that poor Herbie thought he was being yelled at, the dog hanging his head as he morosely headed for the conference table, Jorie would bet to hide. Odelia must have seen, because she scooped the brown pooch up and gave him a pat. "The sooner you get this done, the better." Her eyes narrowed. "I expect an engagement ring on that girl's finger by the end of the day."

BUT AS IT turned out, their plans were interrupted by a surprise visit from a potential client and her fiancé. Ryan had watched as Jorie and his mother drove away, the happy couple in the backseat of the John Deere Mule. It was still overcast and Ryan wondered if it would rain. That would be fitting. Dark and gloomy on the day he picked out a ring.

"Crap," he muttered to himself.

How had his life gotten so out of control?

He'd have gotten Laurel a ring sooner or later. It wasn't as though Laurel was expecting something big and conspicuous. She knew as well as Ryan that this was all a sham. Well, okay, not really a sham, but close enough.

"You look like a horse that's been whipped into a lather."

Ryan looked up, not surprised to see Sam since he'd summoned him to the office.

"Just busy," he hedged. Sam didn't know the truth about his engagement. Nobody knew.

"I ran into Lyle earlier today. Guess he had something special to give her."

Sam pulled up a chair, sitting down in front of him. Ryan hated looking into his eyes. Sam had a knack for looking below the surface, a knack that frankly irritated the hell out of him sometimes.

"Yeah. Her mom's veil."

"So everything's moving ahead?"

That had Ryan looking up sharply. "Yeah, sure. Why wouldn't it?"

"Just wondering." The man leaned back. "You've been moping around here for so many days I've been wondering if you're having second thoughts."

Ryan froze, or at least he told himself to freeze. He

didn't want to give anything away. "Don't be ridiculous," he said quickly.

And all Sam did was lift a brow.

It took an effort to concentrate over the ensuing hour as he and Sam went over invoices, and even more of an effort not to jump up when he heard Jorie and his mother return. They sounded like a herd of elephants coming up the stairs, Jorie all smiles as she breezed through the squeaky door.

"Oh, Sam. There you are," his mother said. "We were just looking for you."

"Ma'am," Sam said, ever formal even though he'd known Ryan's mom for well over half his life.

"I was going to ask you to take Jorie out to the east pasture tomorrow, but now that I think about it, Ryan would be a better choice."

"Excuse me?" he interjected.

His mother ignored him.

"I'll have him take you to what we call the meadow." She smiled in Jorie's direction. "It'll be a trek for her wedding guests, but I think it's exactly what she's looking for. Too bad we didn't have any photos."

"That's my job now," Jorie said, looking at Ryan in a way that made him think she didn't like the idea of spending time with the owner's son any more than he wanted to spend time with *her*. "And there's no reason for Ryan to take me. I'm sure Sam doesn't mind." She smiled in his direction.

"Nonsense. Sam has too much to do."

"And I don't?"

His mom continued to ignore him. It hit him then. This was revenge. Punishment for not putting a ring on Laurel's finger.

"Keep an eye out for other locations we can use in

the future, too." Odelia smiled brightly. "We have a few places that are just stunning. Unfortunately, some of them are miles away."

"Miles?" Jorie glanced between the two of them, though his mother continued to ignore him. Sam was leaning back in his chair, apparently amused at the way his mother was treating him. Clearly, the man had picked up on the tension between Ryan and his mom. "How big is this place?"

"Twenty thousand acres," she said.

The words seemed to break through the dread Jorie clearly felt, dread she couldn't quite conceal, though she tried.

"Twenty thousand," she repeated softly.

"It's been in our family for generations." Odelia's pride was obvious. "We didn't start out with that much, but then my grandfather found oil in the southern pasture. He used the money the oil company gave him to buy up every piece of vacant land he could get his hands on. Over the years we've acquired more. You could ride all the way to Fredericksburg if you wanted to."

Ryan decided he was tired of being ignored. "'Course," he said, "it'd take you a couple days."

"Oil?" Jorie squeaked.

"Of course," his mother said. "We have several wells, actually, they're just way out back so you can't see them." His mother's head turned toward him like a snake on the attack. "And so it's not like Ryan couldn't afford to buy Laurel a ring."

He heard someone choke back a laugh. Sam. "So that's what this is about," his friend murmured after leaning forward a bit. Ryan shushed him with a look.

"I told you, Mom, I'm going. Right now as a matter of fact." He stood, opened a drawer, found his keys inside and crammed them in his pocket. "Jorie. Let's go. Sam, you and I can finish up later."

"You got it, boss."

Jorie clearly didn't want to go, though. Point of fact, she looked like a horse being asked to jump a puddle of water. He didn't know why, but the look bothered him.

"Unless you have something better to do," he added.

"No, no," she said quickly, clearly torn by her desire to avoid him like the plague, and her wish to do as his mother asked. "Like your mom said, I need to go into town, anyway. There's a whole slew of people I need to meet, most of them on this list here." She opened up her own drawer and pulled out a sheet of paper. "I especially want to meet with some of the florists. Our bride has some unusual flowers she'd like in her arrangements. I think I'll have more luck pulling strings if I meet people face-to-face."

His mother pulled her rabid stare away from him, and it was amazing the way her brows went from low and angry to all soft and inviting when she smiled in Jorie's direction. "Don't forget, dear, I still have my contacts from when I was doing arrangements if you can't find anything local."

"I know." Jorie, obviously resigned now, folded up the list and stuck it in her purse. She shot his mom and Sam a smile that lit up her face, and made Ryan look away. "But let me see what I can do first. I also want to meet a few of the catering managers. And the party rental people. It'll take me half a day to get down my list."

Beautiful. That's why he had to look away. The damn woman was a knockout.

"I don't have half a day." He didn't mean to sound

like a jerk, but that sure was the way his words came out sounding.

"Then I'll just do what I can," she said, sending him an apologetic smile that made him feel like even more of a heel because he really hadn't meant to snap at her.

"Let's go." And there he went snapping again.

His mother still shot him a glare as he rose to his feet. This time *he* ignored *her,* snatching his hat from the hook and cramming it onto his head. He just wanted to get this over with. And yes, he knew that was a horrible attitude to have, but he'd begun to feel like Daniel on his way to confront the lions, and he just couldn't see any honorable way out of the whole deal.

It didn't help to hear Sam's softly uttered, "Have fun," as he slipped through the door.

IT WAS LIKE being in the car with a soldier of fortune. The man didn't so much as crack a smile as he started the engine of a big, black Ford truck that probably cost more than a house and smelled like a new purse.

"What kind of ring were you thinking of getting Laurel?" she asked to break the ice.

"I'll know it when I see it."

She couldn't even hear the tires crunch as they drove down the gravel road, the engine was so loud. The day was still overcast and gray, too, the driveway with its white fence along both sides a ribbon of gray painted upon a green canvas. Even though the clouds hung low, it was still the most picturesque landscape she'd ever seen. Horses grazed in the distance, as did cattle, lots and lots of cattle.

"You know, if you'd rather do this alone, you could just drop me off at the first florist shop."

No answer.

"You can pick out Laurel's ring on your own."

"My mom wants you to help."

"Yeah, but I could tell her you weren't comfortable with that." She watched as his hands tightened on the steering wheel, the movement causing his arms to flex beneath the cranberry-colored shirt. "Or not."

"You're going."

She took a deep breath, trying hard to maintain her patience as they drove south toward Fredericksburg, but he made it difficult. It didn't help that each breath she took carried the scent of him. He looked good in that cowboy hat of his. She'd never been one to like the outdoorsy type, and yet she found herself thinking there could be no more virile a sight than a man in tight jeans and work-worn boots. That was the problem. She shouldn't be attracted to a man who snapped at her all the time and drove her nuts in the process, but most of all, a man who was engaged. Clearly, this would be a miserable day...for both of them.

"Look," she said before she could think better of it. "I refuse to spend the next few hours with a Grinch." She swiveled in her seat to face him. "So if you're going to be a jerk, just leave me out of it. We can tell your mother I bowed out, or that I got sick. Whatever. This should be a happy occasion." She swung forward again, muttering, "Instead it's like a darn wake."

He tossed her a look, one that said he couldn't believe she'd talked to him like that. Well, too bad, she silently told him right back.

And then his shoulders slumped.

He reached for his hat with one hand, scratched his forehead, and then grimly gripped the steering wheel again.

"I've been an ass."

"Yes, you have."

"It's the wedding."

"Yes, it is."

She watched his lips flatten, saw his hands grip the steering wheel to the point that his knuckles turned white.

"I just don't want to let Laurel down."

Envy. That was the only word to describe how she felt. "That's very sweet," she said, ordering a smile to appear on her face.

"Like this ring thing. I'm just not certain I really know what she wants."

"Maybe you should have brought her along."

He shook his head so quickly Jorie knew that wasn't an option.

"Or her dad."

He huffed out a breath of derision. "No way."

Okay, so he didn't get along with his father-in-law. Maybe that was the source of some of his tension. Maybe he hadn't liked Lyle visiting her earlier.

"You're perfect," he said, then quickly added, "Perfect to bring along, I mean."

Well, okay then. At least she'd established he didn't secretly despise her. She'd been starting to feel that way. Every time he was near her he acted surly and rude. The question was, why?

She peeked a glance at him.

He didn't feel an attraction, too, did he?

But then she remembered his blush. Remembered the expression on his face when he'd caught her standing there half-naked. Recalled that on the few occasions they'd been together, she'd caught him staring at her. Not in a weird stalker kind of way, just enough times that she'd started to grow self-conscious. And then there was his reaction when he'd touched her thigh.

He's in love with Laurel.

Or was he?

Jorie hardly remembered the rest of the trip. She was so deep in thought it took her a good five minutes to notice they'd reached the outskirts of Fredericksburg, a town that immediately caught her attention with its nineteenth-century buildings, beautifully decorated adobe storefronts and old-fashioned feel.

"This is great," she declared. It was exactly the type of downtown she liked to explore. A variety of stores seemed to welcome visitors in with their covered walkways and huge picture windows. Art galleries, boutiques and restaurants, not all of them sporting covered walkways, sat along Main Street, parking spaces right out front.

"Oh, yeah, great," he echoed. He was back to looking sullen again. "Come on," he said after pulling into a spot in front of a brick building with a wooden overhang. The sign that hung above a covered walkway said Richard's Jeweler. "Let's get this over with."

No. He wasn't in love. His tone of voice said it all.

Well, well, well.

Chapter Nine

"Mr. Clayborne," said a man Ryan didn't recognize, the door tinkling in their wake. "I've been expecting you."

Ryan almost turned right back around again, except his mother would kill him.

He looked up from beneath the brim of his hat in time to see a man the size of Texas slip out from behind a huge, glass counter, one filled with rings and watches and other pieces of jewelry. He wore a dark gray suit that must have cost him a fortune, and not because it was tailored. It must have taken at least ten yards of fabric to cover him from head to toe.

"And this must be your beautiful fiancée," gushed Mr. Richard, or at least that's who Ryan assumed he was. He certainly moved across the hardwood floor with the speed of someone who owned the place. "My, my, my, and what a lucky man you are, Mr. Clayborne."

The man came to a stop atop a giant, black rug with the store's name on it. "I'm William Richard. Welcome to my shop."

"She's not my fiancée," Ryan snapped.

To give him credit, William Richard recovered quickly. "Oh. I do beg your pardon."

"I'm his wedding planner," Jorie explained.

"Ah. Of course you are. Forgive my mistake. I

thought I knew most of the wedding planners in town. You must be new to Fredericksburg."

He smiled at them both, though it was obvious the man was still uncomfortable.

"I am." Ryan watched as Jorie smiled at the man reassuringly. She could make the devil feel home in heaven, he thought. "I'm Odelia Clayborne's new assistant, Jorie Peters."

They shook hands. "Pleasure to meet you, Ms. Peters."

"What a beautiful store you have," she said, looking around. On the walls were clocks, their ticktocks filling the room with sound. "It feels like we've stepped back in time a hundred years."

"The building's been here since the late 1800s," Mr. Richard said, clearly pleased that she'd noticed.

Jorie leaned forward and gave the man a smile meant to set him at ease.

"It's not the first time I've been mistaken for a bride, by the way." She ratcheted up the volume of her smile in a way that would have melted a heart-shaped box of candy. "It must be the color I'm wearing."

She motioned toward the silky, off-white sweater she wore, the one that made her look like a model. Ryan thought she couldn't be more different from Laurel if she tried. Quiet and unassuming. Those were words that fit Laurel. Not Jorie. Laurel wouldn't have said a word to the jewelry store owner, just let Ryan handle the situation. Yet here was Jorie already charming the socks off him. He could tell William Richard appreciated Jorie's words of reassurance, too, and that she had a new fan.

"I can tell Odelia's lucky to have you." He smiled in Ryan's direction. "Mr. Clayborne, your mother gave me specific instructions to pull out only my best pieces. Follow me."

Well, of course she did. His mom couldn't resist meddling even when he'd specifically asked her not to. She loved Laurel like a daughter.

Just as he loved her like a sister.

"I had no idea what size diamond you were looking for so I just pulled out an assortment of shapes and carats." The man slipped behind his counter, returning a few seconds later with a tray of rings that sparkled beneath the canned lighting and caused Ryan's stomach to plummet to his toes.

This was it.

"Jorie, you pick."

Mr. Richard looked up at him in surprise.

Ryan turned away. He had to tell himself not to run, although it felt as if the neck of his shirt had suddenly shrunk.

"Ryan, really," he heard Jorie say. "This is something you should do for yourself."

He took a deep breath, forced himself to unclench his hands.

What are you doing?

Getting married, he firmly told himself, turning to face Mr. Richard who stared at him as if he might suddenly scream obscenities at him. He must look like walking thunder. That's what his mom always said when he was in a bad mood.

"Sorry," he mumbled, though he didn't know who he was apologizing to, Jorie, the shopkeeper or his absent mother. "This whole ring thing just isn't my deal."

The man didn't look convinced.

"Let's start with the basics," Jorie said, and Ryan noticed she had perfectly manicured hands. A ring would look good on her finger. "Do you know what shape diamond you want?"

"Round," he said, though in reality it was the first word to pop into his mind.

"White gold, platinum or eighteen-karat gold?" the shopkeeper asked.

And though he knew he shouldn't do it, he looked at Jorie and tried to envision what *she* would want.

"Platinum."

"Good choice," said Mr. Richard.

Just have her *pick out the damn ring.*

"Size?" the man asked.

"I don't know."

"No problem," said the man. "What about carats. Any idea how big you want to go?"

He peered at the tray of rings in front of him, and even though he told himself it was a damn foolish thing to do he glanced at Jorie again, trying to imagine what she would want.

"Nothing too big," he said. "Something showy, but not too flamboyant."

She was staring at him strangely, as if she knew what was going through his head. But that wasn't possible. She couldn't read minds.

"There," he said, pointing to an oval-shaped ring that sent out sparks of color. "That one with the fancy design on it."

"Ah," said Mr. Richard. "The filigree. Excellent choice."

If he'd picked a ring made of tin, the man would have said the same thing, Ryan thought.

Mr. Richard picked up the ring in question. "Isn't it stunning?" he asked.

Ryan turned toward Jorie. "What do you think?"

"It's beautiful."

She didn't like it. He could tell. Though he barely

knew her, he recognized the little wrinkle between her eyes. The way her lips compressed slightly, only to relax into a make-believe smile.

"What's wrong with it?" he asked.

"Nothing," she said quickly.

"You don't like it. Why?"

Discomfort shone from her eyes.

"Come on. You can tell me."

"Okay, fine. I *don't* like it... I mean I *do*. It's truly lovely." Her eyes grew wistful. "It's just not right."

"How so?"

"Because it's not Laurel."

"Okay, then tell me what *is* Laurel?"

She worried her bottom lip. Ryan watched as her tongue snuck out for a second.

He nearly groaned.

"Nothing too delicate. This ring is fancy, Laurel is... simple. Less...girly."

And she'd nailed her right on the head. Amazing. It must be her training. She was good at picking up on the small details.

"So tell me what you think would work."

"I'm thinking she'll want something elegant, yet practical. Something that won't get damaged when she works around the ranch." She smiled up at him again. "That's why platinum is such a good choice. It's one of the hardest metals."

"She's absolutely right," said the jeweler. "Perhaps you'd like to look at the selection of platinum rings only?"

Ryan lifted his hat, scratched his forehead before saying, "Fine."

Jorie nodded her approval. He had to look away, not that it did any good. He was aware of Jorie standing next to him, of the way she smelled and the warmth of her body—

Stop it.

This was ridiculous, not to mention, sick. He was here to pick out a ring for Laurel, not lust over his mom's new wedding planner.

"Here we go," said Mr. Richard after he rearranged the available selection of rings. "These are your choices." He waved a hand over the right side of the tray where he'd sequestered about ten rings.

Ryan glanced at each of them and decided he hated them all. "You choose," he told Jorie.

"Ryan—"

He began to turn away before he could stop himself from doing otherwise. "You're the professional."

"But still—"

"Please," he said, pausing for a moment. "Pick."

He watched her pretty blue eyes dart over his face, as if searching for clues to what could possibly be going on. Whatever she saw, she must have realized how serious he was because she examined the tray, pointing to a ring with a band of inlayed diamonds and a round center stone that was beautifully cut, yet not too big.

"There," she said.

He watched as Mr. Richard picked up the ring.

And he couldn't breathe.

The hypocrisy of it all. Why had he agreed to do this? Laurel would be okay. Yeah, her dad would lose his mind, but he'd get over it. Surely they didn't need to go through with this charade of a marriage?

"That one's stunning," he heard the jeweler say. "Two carats. Oval cut. Simple, yet elegant."

His stomach churned again, this time to the point

that he suddenly felt ill. He took a step, then another and another. "I'll be right back."

"Ryan?" Jorie called out, concern in her voice.

He kept walking, needing air. God help him, what was he about to do? Did he really want to consign himself to a loveless marriage?

The answer came to him instantly.

No.

"Ryan, wait."

He heard footsteps behind him, and he sped up, pushing through the door so hard the handle stung his palms.

"Darn it, Ryan, stop."

It started to rain. Ryan could hear it on the roof that covered the walkway. He could smell it, too, the scent of wet dirt suddenly filling the air. He didn't know where he was going.

He should have grabbed a coat, he thought, stepping out from beneath the covered walkway and heading toward the neighboring building. His hat only shielded part of his shoulders. Rain left dime-sized spots on the red fabric. He didn't care.

"Hey."

Jorie rushed by him, placed a hand against his chest. "If you don't love her, why are you marrying her?"

The jewelry store must have a walkway covered by tin, that was why he didn't hear her right.

"Believe me, Ryan. The last thing you want to do is marry someone you don't love."

Only he *had* heard her right. She stared up at him, rain dotting her cheeks and nose and lips and God help him, he suddenly felt the urge to kiss her.

"Laurel and I will be just fine."

He started off again, although where he was going, he had no idea. He just needed to walk.

"Why?" she called out after him.

He told himself to ignore her, to pretend as if he didn't understand her question, but against his better judgment he found himself turning toward her.

"Because it's the right thing to do," he said.

He turned away again, headed toward a coffee shop at the end of the street. That's what he needed, a good, strong cup of coffee.

"You got her pregnant, didn't you?"

"No."

"You did, didn't you?" she asked, jumping in front of him once again and grabbing him by the arm.

He told himself to deny it, after all, he hadn't gotten Laurel pregnant. But something about the way she stared up at him, something about what he saw in her eyes. It had him thinking crazy thoughts. "Yeah," he heard himself say. "I did."

And why he did that, he had no idea. Except…maybe he did. Maybe he said it because as he looked into her eyes, he saw kindness there. That, and something else. Something that scared him and had him thinking he needed to scare her off.

"Is that why you're marrying her?"

No, he wanted to say.

"Yes."

He got what he wanted then. The thing he saw in her eyes, he killed it with a single word.

She stepped back from him, hugged her arms around herself, raindrops saturating her face and flattening her hair around her in a way that would have made a lesser woman look horrible, but it was impossible for Jorie to look bad, he'd begun to realize.

"You're an honorable man, Ryan Clayborne," she said softly. "Laurel's lucky to have you."

Chapter Ten

A half hour later they drove home through the oak-stud-
ded countryside in complete silence. Jorie attempted to
engage him once or twice, but his monosyllables made
conversation next to impossible. It was almost a relief when they reached the end of Spring Hill Ranch's
long drive.

"Office?" he asked.

"No," she said. "I'm done for the day."

He didn't say a word, just made the left-hand turn
toward the old ranch house. It was still raining, the
wipers squeaking upon the glass, the quiet whirr of the
truck's heater causing Jorie to grow sleepy. It'd been a
long day. After they'd returned to the shop, Ryan had
played chauffeur while she visited the local florist and a
couple of caterers. Everyone had seemed glad to see her.

Everyone but Ryan.

"Thanks for the ride," she said after he pulled to a
stop in front of his home.

He didn't say anything, just nodded, but he didn't
shut off his engine. Jorie watched the wipers traverse the
glass one more time before opening the truck door. The
arcs the wipers left behind were like colorless rainbows.

"I'll see you tomorrow."

He nodded without a word.

She couldn't get out of his truck fast enough. She waited to hear him drive off, was surprised when he shut off his truck's engine instead. She resisted the urge to turn and look, to see what he was doing. What she wanted to do was get out of her dank clothes. Even though it'd been a forty-five-minute drive back to the ranch, she was still damp from the multitude of dashes in and out of the truck throughout the day. She was tired, too, the stress of everything wearing her out. What she wanted to do was take a shower. Maybe start a fire afterward. She had a fireplace, she thought, dashing for the front door.

He'd gotten Laurel pregnant.

So? she asked herself. It happened. At least Ryan was marrying Laurel.

Unlike her own father—

She quickly quashed the thought.

Ryan was going to be a father, and though he hadn't meant it to happen, she had no doubt he'd do his best when it came to raising his child. He was that kind of man. And the child would have a loving home, and a grandmother who would spoil the child to death.

She couldn't get her key in the door. Her hands shook too badly. Must be the latent memories of her childhood.

"Jorie."

The keys slid from her hands.

"Here."

He came up to her quickly, grabbed the keys before she could.

"Thanks," she said, taking them from him. Yet for some reason she couldn't look him in the eye. She couldn't breathe, either.

"Don't mention any of this to my mom."

She shot him a look of reproach. "Of course not."

He was staring down at her and she spotted it then, the inner misery that was in his eyes. "It's really not what you think."

"No?"

"Laurel and I have an understanding. We'll give our marriage a year, maybe two, and then we'll see what happens."

"What about the child?"

"What do you mean?"

"Are you just going to leave it behind?"

Now it was his turn to stare down at her reproachfully. "Her child will always be taken care of."

Her child. "It's *your* child, too, Ryan."

He half turned, looked off into the distance. The rain made it seem darker than it was, the drops that fell on the roof a staccato beat that for some strange reason, helped to make Jorie feel as if they were the only two people in the world. He was shaking his head, slowly, as if denying to himself that he'd fathered a child.

"It's such a damn mess."

"Yes, it is," she said. "But I respect you for doing the right thing."

"That's just it," he said, facing her again. "It's not me that should be doing the right thing."

She was starting to shiver, she realized, wishing she had a jacket. "What do you mean?"

Again he turned. Again he stared out into the distance, this time without moving, staring watchfully like an animal trying to sense danger.

"The child's not mine."

The words literally rocked her back. "Excuse me?"

"I know I told you it was," he said, hooking his hands in his jeans, shoulders slumped as he faced her again. "But I had to tell you that. In another month, maybe two, it'll be pretty obvious Laurel's pregnant. We don't want anyone to think I'm not the father."

Her teeth had begun to chatter. Outside the warmth of the car, she'd grown cold quickly. "Why? Surely in this day and age people will understand."

"Not Laurel's dad." He rocked his hat back, scratched his forehead, a nervous habit she suddenly realized. "He's as old school as they come. He didn't like Laurel's ex-boyfriend, either. If he were to find out the man left her the moment she told him she was pregnant and wanted to keep the baby, he's apt to hunt him down with a shotgun." He lifted his hands. "No lie."

"And that's somehow your problem?"

She hated to sound cold and callous, but if he was telling the truth, it was the most ridiculous reason in the world to marry someone.

"You have to know Lyle Harrington."

"And what about your mom? You don't think she won't be hurt when she finds out the truth?"

He tipped his head down and didn't move for a moment. "That's the part I didn't really think through," he admitted.

She couldn't see his face, the black hat he wore obscuring it from view.

"I didn't think a lot of this through." He met her gaze again. "I didn't think about my mom...or what might happen if someone came along who I was attracted to."

Though she was chilled to the bone, though her body shook, a warmth seeped through her when she spotted the look in his eyes.

So he did feel it, too.

"Ryan, I—"

"No," he interjected. "Don't say anything. I know this is a lot to swallow. I know you might find it all hard to believe, but you can ask Laurel if you want. I'll tell her I talked to you. You sort of need to know, anyway." He scratched his head again. "Laurel's having a hard time with this, too. She told me about her meeting with you, said she felt horrible, especially when Lyle showed up. She's racked with guilt."

She believed him. It explained so much.

He took a step closer to her. Jorie told herself to move back, that what she saw in his eyes could be dangerous, maybe even forbidden, and yet she didn't move.

"I can't stop thinking about you," he confessed. "And yet here I am with a damn engagement ring in my pocket that I'm supposed to be giving to my bride."

"Ryan—"

He cupped her face with his hands. "I just have to find out."

She froze, told herself again to pull away. But she knew what he wanted.

"Jorie," he murmured.

And so she didn't move away. Didn't do anything other than close her eyes as his head came closer, and then closer still, the cold she'd felt earlier completely gone now.

She felt the warmth of his body first, then the heat of his breath. Something grazed her lips, something hot and yet delicate that pressed against her own lips, at first gently, then harder and harder.

Oh, dear.

Because there was no denying it. Just that one touch and her whole chilled, tired body came alive. The pressure increased even more, and even though Jorie knew she shouldn't, that things had gone far enough, she opened her mouth, groaning as she tasted him for the first time.

Coffee and cream. Sugar and spice…and Ryan. That's what he tasted like, his essence filling her mouth and seducing her to open for him even more.

He pressed her backward at the same time he seemed to lose control, suckling her tongue. She moaned again, suckled him back, so instantly aroused by his taste and his tongue that she wanted more.

He pulled back.

She gasped.

"Oh, damn," he said.

She wiped at her mouth with the back of her hand, realized she was panting, her body trembling for a different reason now.

And then he turned, walking away without a backward glance, Jorie leaned against her front door and nearly slid toward the porch.

"Oh, damn," she echoed softly.

HE DECIDED TO ride.

Even though it was pouring rain, even though his mom told him he was crazy, even though he nearly ran over Jackson in his rush to get out of the barn, he all but dragged his horse out of the barn.

He wanted her.

Their kiss had proven just how much. He led his horse down the long aisle leading to the entrance of the covered arena.

"Be careful," his mom called out from within the shelter of the building, her gaggle of dogs pacing anxiously at her feet. She had her hands on her hips, her gray hair tucked beneath a red cowboy hat. Concern painted shadows upon her face.

"Don't worry about me," he said, urging his horse out into the cold rain before spurring it into a canter.

The drops nearly blinded him. His horse shook its head. He patted the gelding's neck in apology and headed toward his mom's house. There was a trail that went past it that would take him to a place he hadn't been to in a while, a place he used to call his own when he was little. Fort Clayborne. When Laurel was nine he'd told her about it. It'd become their own secret hideaway then, the Harrington ranch bordering their own. It was secluded there, the creek gurgling loud enough to drown out the sound of voices, the trees so thick no one would see him.

A place where he could think.

The churning legs of his horse forced the rain against him harder. He pulled the jacket he'd grabbed from the tack room door close around him, his horse following the path on its own. It wasn't far, though when they were kids it'd seemed like miles. He approached his mom's house, the smaller bridal cottage visible in the distance, remembered happy times when his father had been alive. He'd been killed in a tractor accident when Ryan was ten. Ryan could still remember the day it'd happened, remembered how, even as a young kid, he'd known his life would never be the same again.

What would your dad say about this whole mess?

He'd be proud of him, Ryan quickly reassured himself. Tell him he was doing the right thing. His dad had been close to Lyle Harrington, too. They'd been like brothers, which is why Lyle had become a second father to Ryan. Hell, there'd even been a time when he'd fantasized about Lyle marrying his mother, but the two of them would only ever be good friends. And now he was marrying Laurel and a part of him wondered if it was out of some twisted sense of obligation.

"Damn, fool idea."

He passed his mom's house, rode by the pool in the back, raindrops hitting the water's surface so hard it kicked up a back splash. No lights were on in the bridal cottage, but the building still reminded him of what he strove to forget. It would be dark in a couple of hours, but he didn't let that stop him. He could find his way home with a blindfold on.

It wasn't so bad once he made it to the tree line. Ryan turned left and followed the trail until he hit the creek. Already the rain had turned its sleepy passage into a fast-moving rapid. That was okay. Where he was going the creek never flooded.

The brush thickened. He had to get off his horse at one point. Everything was overgrown, but not to the point that he couldn't make his way to the secluded cove. The water was deeper here, the creek appearing almost serene, but he knew better. He tied his horse up to a tree, his hands numb with cold. But he had something for that, too. His saddle pack contained matches. It wasn't hard to find wood dry enough to burn. He took care to clear a spot, one far enough away from brush that it wouldn't catch fire, not that he had to worry about a fire getting away from him on a day like today.

He enjoyed the sound of the rain on the leaves above his head, enjoyed tending to the fire, watching it grow, adding wood to it until he had a nice-sized little blaze… which must be why he didn't hear the horse and rider approach until it was too late.

"Hey, Ryan."

Laurel.

His mom must have called her in a panic and Laurel, sweet Laurel, had been concerned for her friend. He could see it on her face as she hopped off her horse. She wore a plastic cover over her cowboy hat that turned the black a dusky gray, and a yellow rain slicker that stood out against a backdrop of brush and trees. In a word, she looked *warm,* something he hoped to be soon, he thought, adding another piece of wood to the fire.

"Your mom called." She tied her horse up next to his own.

"Figured as much."

Her raincoat crinkled as she turned to face him. "Said you rode off like a man on his way to a gunfight."

Sounds like something his mom would say.

"Does this have to do with the wedding?"

He didn't answer, just stared into the flames.

She squatted down next to him, leaned in, grabbed a piece of wood and tossed it on the fire. She wore jeans beneath her slicker, her lace-up boots made of leather that were as worn as her saddle.

Rancher's daughter.

That's what Laurel was, unlike Jorie. Hell, he thought, picking up a twig of his own, stripping it of dead leaves and lobbing it onto the flames, he didn't even know where Jorie was born, much less what kind of childhood she'd had.

"You want to talk about it?"

"No."

"If it helps, my dad was grilling me about our engagement, too."

"It's not that."

"Then what is it?"

When he met her gaze, he noticed her head was tilted to one side, long strands of brown hair spilling over one shoulder. Her gray eyes were full of concern mixed in with sadness.

"I had to buy you a ring today."

Her mouth formed into an O. She looked toward the

fire, her eyes seeming to dance from the reflection of the flames.

"Ryan," she finally said. "If you want to back out—"

"No," he said quickly, although that's exactly what he'd come here to think about.

"You don't need to fear my father. Once I explain the truth, he'll understand."

"I said I would marry you and I will."

She leaned toward him again, grabbed another piece of kindling. "Don't sound so excited about it."

He shook his head. "I'm not going to lie, Laurel. I hate deceiving my mom. She's so excited. I thought she was going to kill me when she realized I hadn't bought you a ring. And then today, when I was picking that ring out for you, all I could think was that maybe we were making a mistake."

"Maybe we are," she said, tipping her head up. "That's why maybe we shouldn't do this."

"Your father would disown you, Laurel. You would break his heart. You know it and I know it. He still thinks of you as his little girl. Telling him you're pregnant out of wedlock…"

"He'd get over it."

"No," Ryan said, meaning it. "He's too old-fashioned. Too stubborn."

"So you want to go through with it then?"

No. He didn't want to go through with it at all.

She scooted closer to him, her hand reaching out to cover his own. It was warm. Far warmer than his own.

"You know this might work."

He shook his head.

"We're best friends. Plenty of marriages have started out with less than that."

"We've never even kissed."

"We can change that," she said softly.

He didn't want to.

"Ryan?" she said, her face leaning close to his.

He shot up from the fire. "Not now."

When he glanced back down at her she didn't bother to hide her disappointment. "I'm sorry," she murmured. She covered her belly with her hand. "So sorry to do this to you."

He turned away again, so torn by his loyalty to Laurel and his own personal desires that he felt almost ill.

"Is there someone else?" Laurel asked, standing.

"No," he said quickly, perhaps too quickly.

Laurel didn't seem to notice. The fire snapped. One of their horses snorted. The rain began to lighten up, the sky slowly darkening.

"Ryan," she said, moving closer, "I promise. If this doesn't work out, we can call it quits."

"How long?"

"How long what?"

"For how long do we give this a try?" he asked.

"I don't know, at least until the baby's born."

The noose of commitment slowly tightened around his neck.

"And if I do meet someone else?"

She moved closer, stepped in front of him. "Have you?" she asked again.

"No," he said. "But if I do? You're asking me to be celibate, Laurel, and I'm no monk."

"You wouldn't *have* to be celibate."

"Yes, Laurel," he said firmly. "I would."

She looked away, the flames highlighting her profile. "Then I would hope you could wait, at least as long as we're married."

They weren't married, and still he felt so racked by

guilt that after kissing Jorie all he'd wanted to do was run away. Yet he'd never leave Spring Hill Ranch. And he'd never leave Laurel, not after he'd promised her his name.

He was just that type of guy.

"You have my word I'll never cheat on you as long as we're together."

Though the daylight had waned, he could still see her relief. "Thank you."

He headed toward his horse, his feet sinking into the ground. Once he escaped the shelter of the trees, the drops came down harder.

"Where are you going?"

"Back home." He checked his horse's girth. "I need to help feed."

"You don't have to leave," she said as he swung atop his horse and picked up the reins. "Sam will take over for you tonight."

But there was no sense in hiding anymore. He'd made his decision. He'd committed to Laurel. He would stay committed to Laurel.

"I'll see you back at the ranch," he said, turning his horse away.

"When?" she asked.

"Tomorrow. We have things to discuss. Things related to the wedding."

She was pretty in a wholesome sort of way. A lot of men would be happy with a woman like Laurel. Frankly, if he were honest with himself, when he'd agreed to the marriage he'd sort of thought maybe *he* could be happy with her.

And then he'd met Jorie.

"What kind of things?"

"Just some stuff my mom wants to go over."

"Okay," she said.

He clucked his horse forward, but the gelding had only taken two steps when he pulled him up again. "Oh, yeah," he said, turning back to her. "If we're going through with this, I suppose I better give you this." He reached into his pocket and tossed the ring in her direction, but he didn't wait to see if she caught it. Instead he hightailed it out of there.

Before he changed his mind.

Chapter Eleven

Jorie couldn't sleep.

She rolled over in bed for about the hundredth time and told herself to stop acting like a fool. Ryan would not be sneaking into her house.

Then why'd you wear a pair of frilly underwear and a white tankini to bed?

Because it was warm in the house, she told herself. That's all. He'd made it clear by walking away from her and then disappearing for hours that he considered their kiss a mistake. She did, too.

And still she burned.

Her body came alive at just the thought of his lips on her own, at the memory of what his tongue had done, at the taste of him....

She groaned, tugged the pillow over her head, kicked at her mattress in frustration. Nothing soothed her.

So she lay there.

At some point she must have fallen asleep. She awoke with a start, the sheets tangled around her and the sound of a car revving in the distance. She opened her eyes. The room was the muted gray of morning. And, no, her sluggish mind corrected. That wasn't an engine, it was the sound of her cell phone buzzing atop her nightstand. She'd put it on vibrate.

Where had her bedspread gone? What time was it? She reached for her cell phone. "Hello?"

"Jorie Peters?" someone asked, a female someone.

Jorie reached for the sheet tangled around her feet, dragged it up over her body. "This is she."

"Oh, hey, Jorie. This is Sophia Brandon. We met yesterday. I wondered if you'd had time to scout out some additional locations for my wedding."

Sophia. The bride from yesterday. Was it really only yesterday? It felt like an eternity.

"Actually," Jorie said, "I was hoping to get to that today." She glanced at the time on the clock, only to sit up suddenly. It was nine o'clock.

"Okay, good."

Odelia.

Jorie almost groaned. Was she angry? Not even a week on the job and already she was late.

"I promise I'll get back to you just as soon as possible. Is that okay?"

"Sure, sure," Sophia said. "And I wanted to let you know how much we liked the place. Even with the skies threatening rain, it was still beautiful. I can only imagine what it would be like in the spring."

Jorie could, too, but then she found herself wondering if she'd even be here next spring. She wasn't exactly off to a great start.

Ryan.

She'd have to face him this morning. Goodness. Odelia had asked him to take her out to that lake today.

Please, Lord, let him have already left for the day.

She rang off with Sophia, hopped out of bed, and dressed as fast as she could in a pair of cream-colored slacks and a white blouse. She didn't bother with her hair, just brushed through it, leaving it down. She couldn't believe she'd overslept. Not today. Not when she needed to be at her best to deal with Ryan.

She'd been walking up to the office lately, but she was so late she decided to drive. The only sign that it'd poured yesterday were the puddles that had formed in the gravel road. Her tires splashed through them. She darn near skidded to a halt in front of the big arena.

It was chilly outside the car. She paused for a moment to look for a jacket or sweater or something in the backseat of her car. She should have grabbed one earlier, but she'd been in too much of a hurry.

She heard them first.

Jorie straightened away from her car, cocking her ear toward the arena and the snuffling, snorting, growling sound that came from inside.

Jackson was the leader, rounding the wall to her right like Wile E. Coyote.

"Jackson, no," she said as he ran toward her legs.

The other three rounded the corner next.

"No," she warned them, too, because they weren't slowing down. The big one, Beowulf, galloped toward her like a horse in the Kentucky Derby.

"Beowulf," she commanded. "No."

He wouldn't listen.

She backed away.

He kept coming.

"No," she cried, louder.

He reared back. She thrust her arms out in front of her.

His paws hit her with the force of a battering ram, a silly canine grin on his face as he wrestled her to the ground.

One minute she was on her feet, the next she wasn't. Fortunately, or perhaps not so fortunately, she landed in a puddle of water, or maybe more appropriately a puddle of ooze.

"Beowulf!"

It was Ryan's voice. Jorie had just enough time to recognize it before Beowulf put a big, muddy paw on her chest and then lowered his head.

She covered her face. It didn't help. His big, wet tongue swiped at her cheeks, the other dogs swarming around him, tails wagging, tongues lolling off to the side. Jorie, who would never have thought her day could get any worse, felt the ooze creep into her shirt and pants and any available crevice it could find.

"No," she gasped, trying to shove the dog's face away.

Ryan approached. Odelia and Laurel were right on his heels, Laurel pulling Beowulf off of her while Ryan shooed the other dogs away.

"Oh, my goodness," Odelia cried when she caught sight of Jorie.

She wanted to cry, but not because of the ooze that coated her clothes. No, she wanted to cry because when Laurel grabbed Beowulf's collar, she'd spotted it. The ring. It glittered on her finger like a miniature constellation, proof positive that Ryan had thought nothing about their kiss.

Nothing at all.

"DAMN DOGS," RYAN muttered as he shoved the last of them, Herbie, into the tack room. "Bad dogs," he told the three other canine faces that peered up at him.

Poor Jorie.

She'd looked miserable lying there on the ground, muddy paw prints all over her.

Accusation in her eyes.

When he returned, his mom was trying to clean her up. So was Laurel. Jorie waved off their assistance.

"You look like a mud wrestler," he heard his mother say.

"I think your clothes are ruined," Laurel added.

"I'm okay," she said, though it was clear that she was not. "And if I hadn't overslept none of this would have happened. I would have walked up here as usual and the dogs wouldn't have come running at the sound of my car."

"Laurel, maybe you can get us some towels," his mom said. "There's a bunch beneath the sink in the bathroom upstairs."

"No, no, that's okay," Jorie said quickly.

She had tears in her eyes.

And though he tried to tell himself otherwise, he knew it wasn't because of the mud. Walking away from her last night, it'd hurt her. By now she'd probably spotted Laurel's ring, and the sight of it had been a stab to her heart.

Damn.

"I'm going to head back to the house," she said. "Go change."

"Oh, Jorie," his mom said, eyes wide. "I feel just horrible. I swear I'm sending those dogs for obedience training."

"They're just clothes," Jorie murmured.

"Yeah, but I think Laurel was right. Your clothes are ruined. Ryan will drive you back to your place. Don't get your car all muddy inside."

"No."

His mom froze. So did Ryan. The word had been a pistol crack of rejection.

"Don't be embarrassed," his mom said. "It's not your fault my dogs knocked you down."

He watched Jorie suck in a breath, one that clearly gave away how close to tears she was. "I just want to go home."

His mom drew back, shot him a look of helplessness, then patted Jorie on the back. She must have touched some mud because he saw her wince, then glance at her hand. "Of course you do, dear." She turned toward him. "Ryan, go get the Mule."

"Really, Mrs. Clayborne, that's not necessary—"

"Ryan, go!"

Ryan went. The Mule was only parked around the corner, but Jorie was trying to climb into her own car when he returned. His mom was holding her back like a wrestler pulling someone off the ropes.

"Here he is." She hooked her arm through Jorie's. "Ryan will take you to your place and then bring you back here."

She didn't want to go with him, that much was obvious. His mother, however, all but dragged her toward the passenger side of the Mule. Jorie obviously didn't feel comfortable enough to argue.

"Take your time," his mother said as Jorie climbed inside.

He took off the moment Jorie closed the door. She had to clutch at the handle, but she didn't say anything in protest. Instead she just sat there as he drove away from the barn, and he caught a glimpse of his mother and Laurel—who'd returned with the towels—in the Mule's rearview mirror. He told himself silence was good. Conversation wasn't necessary. It wasn't as if he owed her an explanation or anything.

You shouldn't have kissed her last night, bud.

Okay, fine. Yes, he knew that. He just didn't know what the hell to say to her. "Sorry" seemed so damn inadequate. He'd just been so overcome with curiosity. Felt a need to know if there was something there.

Boy, howdy, had he gotten an answer.

"How did Laurel like her engagement ring?"

He glanced over at her, admitting that even with mud in her hair and paw prints staining her blouse, she was still frickin' gorgeous.

"She loved it," he lied. Truth be told, he hadn't hung around to find out what Laurel had thought about it, although she sure hadn't wasted any time coming over this morning and showing it off to his mom.

That's not fair.

He'd *asked* her to come over. She'd just been pretending to be thrilled about the whole thing. He knew that. Thank God his mother hadn't picked up on the tension between the two of them.

He pointed the Mule between the hay barn and the maintenance shed and searched around for something to say, something that would break the silence that hung between them like an undisturbed tomb.

"I had to do it." He didn't know where the words came from, but once they were out, he felt immediate relief. "I followed you to your porch because I wanted you to know the truth about Laurel and me." He wished they could stop. Hated the way he had to focus on driving instead of looking into her eyes. He would be an even bigger ass if he forced her to sit there in her mud-stained clothes. "There's just something about you—"

"Stop." She held up a hand. "Just stop."

"I know it's no excuse." He studied her for as long as he dared while driving. She was peering out her window, her face too far in profile for him to read. "I know it was wrong."

But I just couldn't resist.

The words were there, unspoken, but there.

"Do you love her?"

His stomach flipped. "I answered that question last night."

Out of the corner of his eye, he saw her turn toward him. "Yet you still asked her to marry you."

They were traveling down the hill that led to the old ranch house, the wedding barn off to their right, and he knew he was going to lose her, that she'd disappear inside the house and think of a reason not to return to the office with him. She'd avoid him from here on out, too, except on those days when he worked in his office and she'd be forced to spend some time with him.

"I don't know how to explain this to you." He shook his head. "I told Laurel I would take care of her. I can't back out of that now."

"Why not?"

Did she *want* him to back out? Had their kiss actually meant something to her? He glanced over at her, trying to read her eyes, but she was like a folded up newspaper. He couldn't even glimpse the headlines with her face partially turned away.

"Because her father, Lyle, is the closest thing to a father I've ever had. Because Laurel is a friend in trouble. Because she has nobody else but me."

"She has a father who loves her, and a second family in you and your mother. She would be okay."

She didn't know Laurel very well if she thought that. She hadn't been there on that night when she'd been in hysterics, Thad's note clutched in her hands, a pregnant Laurel begging him to help her out, just for a while, just until the baby was born. And it'd seemed so simple then, so sensible.

"I can't change the way things are."

They'd made it back to her quarters and Ryan pulled to a stop in front. She didn't hesitate in getting out, not that he blamed her. She had to be miserable in her soggy, muddy clothes. But she paused for a moment after slipping out of the vehicle.

"Can't you?" she asked him, with Ryan looking full into her eyes.

And then she was gone.

Chapter Twelve

At least he'd driven away, Jorie thought, turning away from her window and stripping out of her clothes. It took her twenty minutes to take a quick shower and change, this time into jeans and a light brown sweater in case the dreaded dogs were still around. She pulled her wet hair into a ponytail, glancing out the window one more time to ensure Ryan hadn't returned. She wouldn't have been surprised if Odelia had sent him back for her.

She hadn't. Thank goodness.

With one last glance in the mirror, she stepped out onto the porch. It was as though she'd traveled back in time. She remembered Ryan's lips. Recalled his taste. Remembered how he felt up against her.

Jerk.

So what if he'd kissed her and then gotten engaged the same night? Typical man. Couldn't be trusted. Her mom would have told her that if she'd been alive.

"Whatever," she firmly told herself, tipping her head back to the sunshine. Hard to believe less than twenty-four hours ago it'd been pouring rain. The air smelled freshly washed, the sun warming her damp hair.

Ryan's ATV was nowhere to be seen when she approached the arena. She cocked her head and listened for Odelia's pack of dogs. Fortunately, they seemed to be MIA, too, as Jorie climbed the steps to the offices two at a time.

"There you are." Odelia's smile was wide and welcoming as Jorie walked in, door hinges squeaking behind her. "And you look much better."

"I feel much better," Jorie said, her mood improving when she noticed Ryan wasn't around. "Odelia," she said, taking a seat at her desk. "I'm so sorry I was late this morning."

Her boss waved a hand in front of her face. "Oh, nonsense. Everyone oversleeps once in a while."

"Yeah, but none of this would have happened—"

"Stop," Odelia interrupted, lifting a hand. "It wasn't your fault. It was those damn dogs of mine. I swear I'm going to find new homes for them."

"No," Jorie gasped. "Don't do that."

Odelia shook her head and smiled. "Kidding, my dear. I would never do that. But I will take greater care to keep them contained. Heaven forbid one of our customers arrives at the ranch only to be knocked on their bottom."

She had a point.

"Speaking of customers, did Sophia call you?"

"She did." Jorie hunted on her desk for the woman's file. "I was hoping you might be able to drive me around the property today, instead of Ryan."

"Actually, I have a surprise for you. Something to cheer you up."

Jorie jerked her gaze upward.

"You get to go on a horse ride."

"No."

Odelia leaned back in surprise. "Why not? You're even dressed appropriately. Speaking of which, I really wish you wouldn't wear such fancy clothes. Not that there's anything wrong with what you usually wear," she said quickly. "You always look stunning, I just think it makes more sense to work in jeans. This is Texas. We're not fancy like Georgia."

Funny how little she'd thought of Georgia and her office back there. Then, too. That's exactly why she'd moved away—so she wouldn't have to drive by it and constantly be reminded of her failure.

"I don't really own many pairs of jeans."

"Well then." Odelia's smile grew wide. "We'll just have to go out and get you some. I love shopping."

"Odelia, no. You don't have to do that. And if driving me around the ranch is too much for you, I can have one of the other ranch hands take me around, there's no need to bother Ryan. Maybe Sam. Or maybe I could drive the Mule myself."

"Don't be silly. I told you before that you need to get more comfortable with horses. Heaven forbid you're asked to hold the reins for one of our brides. What would you do? That's why this is so perfect. You'll discover how wonderful horses are. That way, you can sell the experience to our brides."

Sell it? Horses? Wonderful.

"I really don't think it's a good idea."

"Now, now. One of the things you'll learn about me, Jorie, is that I firmly believe in trying new things. I'm going to insist you do this. After all, you never know. You might find you have a passion for horses."

She would never have a passion for horses. She wanted to tell Odelia exactly that, except her new boss seemed so earnest about the whole thing.

"What if I fall off?"

It was a Hail Mary. A last-ditch effort to get her to change her mind.

Odelia dismissed her concerns with a snort.

"We only own quarter horses, honey. Believe me. They don't have a mean bone in their bodies. You'll do fine. And trust me when I say horseback is the best way to see the ranch. It's kind of a long ride out to the lake, but it's worth it. I've never seen prettier country-side than ours."

Jorie wondered if she felt bad about the dog incident and this was Odelia's way to make it up to her. With horses. She probably thought Jorie was secretly excited.

"When?"

A smile bloomed upon Odelia's face like a rose in winter. "Why not right now?"

Jorie groaned inwardly. Clearly, Odelia was delighted by her own idea, so much so that Jorie knew she was doomed.

Doomed to spend half a day with Ryan.

"Damn, stupid, foolish idea," Ryan grumbled as he tossed a saddle onto Belle's back. He was in one of two side-by-side groom stalls in the middle of the long barn aisle. Across from him, on the other side of a pipe panel rail, the arena sat empty. His mom preferred to ride her show horses in the evening after work, which is what she was doing now, leaving him to deal with Jorie.

"The woman doesn't even know how to ride," he muttered to himself.

"No, I don't."

He turned, the girth he'd just picked up slipping from his hands. "Didn't see you there."

"No." She lifted her chin. "I guess you didn't."

She'd changed, although whether she'd done so before or after his mom had ordered the two of them to go on a ride together, he had no idea. She wore jeans and a brown sweater that was the same color as hot chocolate and that hugged every curve.

He looked away.

"If it's any consolation, I don't want to do this any more than you do."

He leaned down, grabbed the two-inch-wide leather strap and stood up again. He could hear horses rustling about in their nearby stalls. The smell of pine shaving filled the air.

"No," he said. "It's not."

He fished the strap through the ring on the saddle, then pulled it taught. Damn it. The girth needed to be shortened on the other side. He ducked underneath one of the two ties that kept the horse inside the grooming stall, the rubber mats beneath his feet masking his footsteps.

"Can I help?"

He let out a breath, forced himself to glance in her direction. "No," he said before moving back to the left side of the horse.

She'd pulled her hair back in a ponytail. She had so much thick, blond hair, he wondered how it stayed in one place. Her almond-shaped eyes looked even more so with her hair pulled back.

Damn his mother for making him do this.

"What's its name?"

"Belle," he said sharply, once again fishing the girth through the ring.

"Is she nice?"

"All of our horses are nice."

He already had his horse tacked up in the groom stall next to Belle's. He'd been planning on riding out to check the condition of the ground. It was getting close to the time of year when they moved the cows to their winter pasture, but it might be early yet. Depended on the length of the grass back there.

"Hand me that bridle there," he said, finishing up with the girth and pointing to the rack of bridles behind him.

"Which one?"

"The broken bit with the silver shank."

"Broken?" she asked, clearly horrified. "You're making me use a broken one?"

He shook his head. "Here's your first lesson in horse riding. When a bit is in two pieces, it's called broken, or a snaffle. It doesn't mean it's broken." He grabbed the bridle in question, showed her what he meant. "See?"

"Oh," she said. "But I warn you, I'm never getting on a horse again so you really don't need to explain all this."

She was serious. He could see it in her eyes. For some reason it made him want to laugh. He'd never met a woman who didn't like horses. To be honest, most of the time they at least pretended an interest. He couldn't stand women like that. In his experience women would say and do anything to try and garner his interest, all because he was a Clayborne. "Rich," he'd overheard one woman say.

Whatever.

He slipped the bridle on Belle's head. "Come on," he said when he was finished. "I'll show you how to get on."

"Can't wait," he heard her mutter.

And despite the turmoil he felt, he almost laughed.

"Stand atop that mounting block." He pointed to a

wooden box with steps built into the side. "I'll bring her up alongside of it."

"Can't you keep right on going? Set the animal free. Tell Odelia she ran away and there's no other horse I can ride."

"No," he said, biting back a smile. "Just throw your leg over and slip onboard."

"Nice horsey," she said, patting its neck like a football player did a fellow linebacker, but when she made the sign of the cross, he let the smile slip free, even felt a puff of laughter slip past his lips.

"Pick up the reins once you get onboard."

"*If* I get onboard," she muttered.

"Go on."

He had to give her credit. Despite having severe reservations, she mounted the horse, although flopped was a more accurate description.

"That was graceful."

"Bite me," she said, picking up the reins.

He out-and-out chuckled, though he told himself not to. He should not encourage her sassiness, but compared to Laurel's compliant attitude, it was a welcome relief. Sometimes Laurel's meek attitude drove him nuts.

He shut down the thought.

"I'm going to get on my own horse. Don't move."

"You're leaving me?" she asked, pretty blue eyes wide.

"Just for second."

"I want down."

"Go ahead and get down," he called over his shoulder, moving to the side of his sorrel gelding and checking the girth before grabbing his horse's bridle.

"I can't get down." She looked around her as if contemplating a flying dismount. "Not without some help."

"Just stay put." He picked up a spade bit with silver conchos up the side of the leather headstall. "I'll be there in a sec."

"And if the horse bolts? What then?"

"As long as you don't kick her in the sides, she's not going to do anything."

When he glanced back up at her, she had the wide eyes of a doe startled by hunters. He felt pity for her then. She really didn't like this. He paused in the midst of buckling the throat latch. His horse tried to rub on his arm, but he pushed it away.

"Jorie, I promise you you'll be fine." He finished buckling. "I would never let anything happen to you," he said, patting his horse's neck.

She met his gaze. Something flashed between them, something personal and intimate that warmed his insides—though it had nothing to do with horses.

Shit.

His hands shook as he went back to doing up the bridle. "Let's go," he said, hooking his hand on a rein and leading his horse forward.

All he wanted to do was get this over with.

Quickly.

Chapter Thirteen

True to his word, Belle had taken good care of her. They rode through two different pastures, one ringed by a white wooden fence and the other ringed by rust-colored metal posts with some kind of half-inch-thick wire between. Eventually they reached the tree line, and Jorie admired the massive oaks that dotted the landscape, their long shadows staining the ground a darker green. They rode along a path, one marked by cow prints and their pudding-like poops that made Jorie grimace. They'd have to do something about that if they were to have wedding guests hike all the way out here.

If she were honest, though, the ride was almost pleasant. The smell of wet leaves filled the air. Occasionally a branch would drip a splash of yesterday's rain. She didn't mind. Ryan made sure she stayed out of trouble. If she hadn't been so damn terrified she might have actually enjoyed herself.

Gradually the trees grew denser, though the path remained wide. They began to climb a small incline. Jorie gasped when they reached the summit. A view like none other greeted her at the top.

"You think this'll work?"

She gazed around in awe. A lake was nestled in the middle of a small valley. Trees framed the edge, sometimes right up to the water's edge, other times hanging back and allowing for a pebbled shoreline. The sun left a zigzag streak of neon light upon its surface. It looked so serene, the water's surface so smooth that beyond the slash of the sun's light, a blue-ribbon-colored sky was reflected upon its surface.

"I think Sophia will love it." She shifted in the saddle. "I think other brides will love it, too."

Ryan was resting his arm on his saddle's horn, the epitome of a Western cowboy as he sat there in his jeans and cowboy hat.

"My mom wants to ferry guests out here by horse-drawn carriage."

"I know," she said. "She told me, but I think it's a little unrealistic right now. The trail out here would have to be widened, and you'd need fifty carriages to get everyone out here in time to watch the bride get married."

They'd settled into a sort of truce on the way out, Jorie realized. She hadn't mentioned his engagement and Ryan hadn't mentioned the kiss. That was good. As far as Jorie was concerned, it was all in the past. Ryan was marrying Laurel and it was up to her to give him the most spectacular wedding she could think of. A wedding Jorie would love for herself.

"Did you want to take some pictures?"

She straightened suddenly. "I didn't bring a camera."

"Never fear," he said, riding toward her while he reached behind him into a saddlebag that held bottled water, too. "My mom told me to pack one."

Thank you, Odelia.

"I'd like to get down if you don't mind," she said.

She didn't think she could juggle the reins and a camera, not on a horse. Plus, she wanted to get closer to the water's edge and she didn't think her horse would like that.

"I'll help you down."

He jumped off so quickly she felt a stab of envy. He was like one of those damn Western stunt riders.

"Just swing your leg out of the stirrup and slide down."

Easier said than done. She realized quickly that her right leg felt like lead and that swinging one's leg over the back of a horse wasn't as easy as it looked.

"Don't be afraid."

She wasn't afraid. She just didn't know what to hold on to and where to put her left leg. Did she keep it in the stirrup? Take it out?

"Here." He tapped her. She glanced down. Before she knew what he was about, he reached up and clutched her sides, began to tug her down.

"Hey."

He pulled her off balance to the point that she had no choice but to fall into his arms, his body blocking her own. He pulled her up against him once her feet hit the ground and just like that, it all came back to her. Every delicious, naughty, erotic sensation he'd aroused.

He let her go. She almost fell, would have if not for the hand she put out, grateful for the saddle that she momentarily clung to.

"Sorry," he said.

Was he apologizing for touching her? Or for something else?

Ignore him. Ignore the memories his touch evoked. She turned toward the lake again, realized she only held one rein, and then used that as an excuse to move away. She picked up the other one that hung toward the ground.

Get it together, Jorie.

"Will you hold the horse while I go take a picture?"

He didn't immediately answer, and Jorie discovered he was staring down at her, hands flexing, his eyes momentarily flickering with something he worked hard to snuff out. He couldn't quite manage the task, however.

"Here." He held out his hand. The camera was in it. She quickly grabbed it.

"Hand me your reins, too," he ordered.

Her heart pounded. She knew why. He'd touched her. It was brief. It was meant to be impersonal, yet she couldn't deny it'd affected her.

She clutched the camera and told herself she was here to do a job, not think about Ryan.

Engaged, she all but yelled at herself, turning and focusing on the scenery around her. She examined the camera, trying to figure out how to turn it on. It was digital, but not one she was familiar with.

"It's on the top," he said. "To the right."

Ah. The thing switched on. She quickly peered at the digital display, snapped a shot.

"There's a place I was thinking would work great for a wedding. Follow the path to the shoreline. It's to the right."

He led both horses toward her. How he did that—felt so comfortable with a horse on either side of him—Jorie didn't know. One of them snorted. She jumped. He lifted a brow.

"Easy for you to smirk," she said. "You were probably born in the saddle."

He shook his head, and though she didn't mean to do it, she still found herself admitting he was one handsome cuss of a man. Laurel was a lucky woman in more ways than one because, man, could he kiss—

Stop.

"Not exactly born, but horses have always been a big part of my life."

"Lucky you," she heard herself say, her frustration with herself leaking into the tone of her words.

"Don't tell me you didn't have pets when you were growing up?"

"I would hardly call a horse a pet, and my mom considered herself lucky to feed the two of us. Pets were out of the question."

Yet she'd always wanted one.

"Not even a cat?"

"Not even a gerbil."

He didn't say anything. She glanced over at him in time to see him shake his head. "That's sad. Everyone should have a dog of their own."

"You have four."

"Now." He glanced down, jumped over a little hole in the dirt path, saying, "Watch yourself on the way down," before adding, "And don't mistake Mom's Mutts for my own."

The laugh escaped her lips before she could clamp down it down. "Mom's Mutts. That's what you call them?"

"It's appropriate, don't you think?"

"I was actually thinking along the lines of Odelia's Ogres."

He laughed, too. "Brat's not so bad."

"He ate my quiche."

"Yeah, but he told me later he was sorry about that."

She found herself on the verge of laughing again. How did he do that? How could he make her feel such lows...and such highs?

He stopped at a nearby tree and slung the reins of the

two horses over a limb. He didn't tie them, just wrapped them a few times.

When he turned back to her, he was smiling, too, the water in front of him catching his eyes and turning them more blue than green.

"Come on over this way," he said.

They lapsed into silence as he guided her toward the water's edge, the peace and tranquility of the area soothing her frayed nerves. Jorie inhaled a deep breath. What she wouldn't have given to grow up in a place like this, a place where she could run and escape her mom's latest and greatest boyfriend.

Something of what she felt must have shown on her face because he asked, "I take it you and your mom must have had it pretty hard."

She didn't answer.

"How old were you when you lost your dad?"

"We didn't lose him," she answered. "He lost us."

They'd reached the area he'd been talking about, Jorie could tell, and he was right. It was gorgeous, a meadow stretching away from the shoreline, a ring of trees surrounding it.

"How old were you when he left?"

"He left before I was born."

He'd paused by the shoreline. Jorie turned back to face him, crossing her arms in front of her, and attempted to change the subject.

"Sophia will absolutely love this. I just don't know how we'd get her out here—or her guests."

"He left before you were born?"

"Yes," and the irony wasn't lost on her. Laurel had found herself in the exact same situation as Jorie's mother, only Laurel had a knight in shining armor. Lucky girl.

"And you haven't seen him since?"

"Not once." She spun in a slow circle. "We could put the altar here. Maybe one made of wood. A trellis with some type of climbing vine."

"She never married?"

"Oh, she married," Jorie answered. "Twice. She gave up on the whole marriage thing when her second marriage fell apart." She kicked at the dirt. "Do you think we could put down some sod here?"

"You'd have to figure out a way to water it, and keep the cows out of it." He glanced around. "And you'd need a lot of sod. Is your mom still alive?"

"No. The cows will be a problem, too."

"When did she die?"

Darn it. She wished he would just drop the issue. "Five years ago, when I was twenty-three. We'd have to do some serious cleanup for this to work."

"We could do a hayride."

It took her a moment to follow his line of thinking.

"I'm sorry about your mom, by the way."

"Don't be. She was a victim of her own circumstances. She died blaming the world for her troubles."

But mostly me.

"That's too bad."

Change the subject, Jorie.

"By 'hayride' you mean to get the guests out here, yes?"

"Yeah. One of our flatbed trailers could be converted. We could pull it with some horses."

She felt excitement fill the void his questioning had evoked. "That's a great idea. How many people do you think would fit on a trailer?"

Thank God he'd changed the subject.

"If we use hay bales as seats, probably around thirty, maybe even forty."

"Could you set up more than one trailer?"

"Sure, but you'd have to talk to my mom about buying the teams of horses." He smirked. "Not that she'll mind buying more horses."

She nodded. "It's a great idea, Ryan. I bet Sophia's wedding guests would love it, too. An authentic Western wedding. Do you think we could get it done by spring?"

"Sure."

"It'll be a dream wedding."

A fish broke the surface of the water, drawing their attention.

"That's important to you, isn't it?" he asked.

"What?"

"Giving brides their dream."

How perceptive of him. "Every girl deserves at least one day in her life that's perfect."

"Because so little of your life has been perfect."

"Excuse me?" she asked, the glare from the sun momentarily blinding her as she turned to face him.

"It's all an act, isn't it?"

She lifted a hand to shield her eyes. He stood there, blue-green eyes unblinking.

"The way you dress. The fancy hairstyles. Even the way you talk. You've worked hard to tame your Georgian accent. It's still there, but you've softened the edges, made it sound genteel."

It was like hearing her fortune told, a fortune that sounded eerily familiar. "I don't know what you're talking about."

He closed the distance between them. She hated that her stomach curled in on itself the closer he drew near. Hated that once again she found herself admiring his stunning blue-green eyes. Hated that she loved the way he smelled, even when she had no business noticing that smell.

"But you do," he said gently.

She couldn't breathe for a moment.

"What were those stepfathers like, Jorie?"

"Okay, that's enough." She lifted a hand. "I didn't come out here to be psychoanalyzed. You happen to be way off the mark, by the way, but it doesn't matter because I'd rather focus on all the work we have to do out here. Will we need to hire a private contractor? Or do you have enough ranch hands to do the work?"

Liar. He'd hit the nail square on the head. She just wished she knew how he'd been able to read her so perfectly.

"We can hire whoever you need." He took another step closer. "That's what you do, isn't it? You think your way through a problem. It's how you've survived."

Yes, it was. It's how she'd made it through the past year. She'd lost her business and her self-esteem in one fell swoop. It'd taken her months to figure out what to do. Thank goodness she'd had enough savings to make it through, although it'd been just barely enough to get her to Texas. Now here she was, starting over again, and the last thing she needed was some silver-spooned cowboy prodding her past.

And stealing kisses.

"I enjoy my work," was all she said when she realized he was still waiting for an answer.

"You solve your own problems."

It was her turn to read into his words, her turn to catch the wistful edge of his tone.

"Life is what you make of it," she said.

"Even when that life throws you a curveball."

"Exactly."

He was referring to Laurel, to how Laurel was counting on him to solve all her problems. He was wishing Laurel was more independent, more like *her*.

The realization would have made her feel proud but for one thing. She was so overcome with envy that she could scarcely breathe. Laurel was lucky to have him. She wished she'd had someone she could lean on. Someone that could be counted on to do the right thing.

She wished Ryan was hers.

Chapter Fourteen

They seemed to make it back to the ranch in half the time. Ryan was grateful for that because being in Jorie's presence was getting harder and harder to bear. He liked her. He was attracted to her. He wanted her.

"Use the mounting block to get down," he ordered when they made it back to the arena, the horses nickering in welcome.

She didn't say anything, just as she hadn't said a whole lot on the way back to the ranch. Not that words needed to be said. There'd been a whole unspoken conversation after the words they'd shared by the lake.

"Whoa," he told his horse, slipping off in time to watch Jorie climb down from Belle—and *climb* was an appropriate word. Her clumsiness was something that might have made him laugh—if he hadn't been in such a sour mood.

"What do I do with her?" she asked.

"Just wrap her reins around the top rail there." His mom was nowhere to be seen which meant she was probably up in the office, answering phone calls and tending to the business that Ryan knew would drive him more and more crazy as time went on.

Sod in the west pasture. And irrigation to water that sod. And vines. Oh, and let's not forget the trellis.

"Thanks for the ride," she said.

He didn't answer, just went about his business, which must have suited her just fine. When he looked up from ungirthing his horse, she was gone.

Thank God.

He'd wanted to touch her out there by the lake. Wanted to pull her into his arms and tell her how much he admired her fortitude. Except he couldn't, and it wasn't because of his engagement to Laurel. Even if he wasn't engaged he'd give a woman like Jorie a wide berth. They weren't the settling down type and he needed a woman that would be a partner, a woman like Laurel, as mismatched as they were. That's probably why he'd agreed to marry her. Laurel knew the deal. She knew what it meant to be a rancher's wife. Jorie would never be happy stuck in Texas on the ranch. This was a temporary stop for her, no doubt about it.

"The last time I saw you look so grim, hay prices had climbed to twenty-three dollars a bale."

He paused with his hands on the saddle, having just about jumped out of his skin. "Mom, I'm beginning to think you like to scare the crap out of me."

"I didn't mean to sneak up on you, son," she said admonishingly. "You were so deep in thought I doubt you'd have heard a tractor."

He pulled the saddle off his horse, which is what he'd been about to do when she'd walked up and startled him.

"I'm trying to get these horses untacked if you hadn't noticed."

"Why don't I untack Belle for you?"

"Because I can do it." He hefted the saddle into his arms, heading toward the tack stall. He wasn't thinking straight, which is why he opened up the door even though he knew his mom had locked the canine terrorists in there.

"Damn it," he shouted as first one and then another and another came piling out, so fast it was hard to tell which was which. Except for Beowulf. He lumbered along. Apparently he'd expended all his energy knocking Jorie onto her keister.

"Why'd you let them out?" his mom called. Ryan looked down the aisle in time to see Belle's rear end disappear into the groom stall.

"I told you I'd untack Belle," he yelled back.

Jackson just about lost traction rounding the corner of the groom stall so quickly. Ryan shook his head and went to put the saddle away. When he made it back to the groom stall, he was just in time to take Belle's saddle from his mom's arms.

"And I told you I'd help," she said.

"Don't you have work to do or something?"

"My, we're in a bad mood, aren't we?"

He made another trip to the tack room, one of the dogs, Herbie, nearly tripping him along the way.

"Damn dogs," he muttered.

His mom met him in the barn aisle.

"You want to tell me what's wrong?"

"Wrong?" He played innocent. "What makes you think there's something wrong?"

His mom squinted up at him. She hated the fact that he was so much taller than her, but that wasn't what made her frown up at him now.

"You've been in a stinky mood since the moment Laurel came in this morning to show me her ring."

"No, I haven't," he said, picking up a brush from a box hanging on a nearby wall. He brushed at his horse's sweat marks a little harder than was necessary, his horse tossing its head and pinning its ears in protest.

"Did you and Laurel fight last night? Is that why I didn't see you until this morning?"

"I gave her a ring. What more do you want from me?"

He winced. Sure enough, his mom pounced on the words.

"You don't want to marry her, do you?" And she sounded horrified. "Dear Lord, Ryan, is that what's bothering you? Why you didn't buy her a ring until I all but forced you into it? You *are* having second thoughts, aren't you?"

Deep breath. Do not let her see you sweat.

But, damn it, he hated lying. Hated it more than anything he'd ever had to do in his life.

"Don't be ridiculous," he said, hoping he sounded convincing. "Of course I want to marry her."

Silence. A horse bumped into a wall. The sound echoed through the arena.

"You're lying."

He hadn't looked in her direction on purpose, hadn't wanted his mom to look into his eyes. Ever since he was three years old she'd been able to tell when he was lying. She'd be able to tell now if he dared to look in her direction.

"I'm not lying."

Yes, you are.

"I'm just busy. The last thing I needed to do was take Jorie on a trail ride."

His mom ducked under the cross ties that held the horse in place. He saw her do it out of the corner of his eye, felt panic set in when he realized she was going to force him to look at her.

"Ryan Clayborne, you answer my question right now."

"What question?"

She stepped in front of him, grabbed him by the shoulders, something that wasn't easy to do given their difference in height.

"Are you in love with Laurel?"

He didn't want to look down at her, but he knew if he didn't his mom would take that as an answer.

"Of course I am," he said. And he meant it. He really did love Laurel…as a sister.

Whatever she saw in his eyes, it must have reassured her because she let him go. She didn't look satisfied though. She looked worried.

"Is it the marriage thing? The 'till death do you part?'"

"Mom," he said, and this time he was the one to gently clutch her arm, although only with one hand. "You're worrying about nothing. Just do me a favor, will you? Concentrate on the wedding."

She held his gaze, eyes so like his own staring up at him unblinkingly.

"I was thinking the spot you picked out with Jorie today would be perfect."

His hands fell to his side. "Are you crazy? It'll take weeks to do what needs to be done out there."

"I'll hire a crew. And a contractor to cut us a road. I might have some trouble finding us a team of horses, but we can use a tractor to pull people along, worst case."

"We'll need at least *two* teams to get all our guests out there."

"Speaking of which, Jorie needs Laurel's guest list. She wants invitations to go out this week. She's worried we're not giving people enough time to RSVP."

He went back to grooming his horse, thankful he'd distracted her with talk of the wedding.

"I'll tell Laurel to call Jorie."

"And you? Is there anyone in particular you want to invite?"

"Nope."

"No one?"

"I'm going to leave it up to you." He shot his mom a smile meant to throw her off the scent even more. She was back to studying him closely.

"What about the wedding party? Who's going to be your best man?"

He hadn't given it a thought, but he said the first name that came to mind. "Sam."

"Sam, what?"

They both turned as the man in question came into sight. "I'm ready to move those pipes out to the south pasture."

"Great," Ryan said.

"Now, what's this about me doing something?"

Ryan shook his head, feeling like a putz for dragging one of his best friends into the whole charade.

"I need you to be my best man."

Sam's dark eyes seemed to darken further. "Really?"

"Really."

Sam wasn't much of an emotional man, but Ryan was pretty certain he saw a glimmer of pride in his eyes.

"I'd be honored."

And for some reason, the words made Ryan feel even worse.

His mom stepped out of the stall. "Good. That's settled. Next I'm going to get with Laurel to find out who she plans to invite. In the interim, I'll see what I can do about getting the lake ready in time. We might have to deal with the weather, but we can always just play it by ear, too. Have the barn ready as a backup or something."

She was back to smiling, her joy in planning the event evident. Ryan had to look away.

"It'll be beautiful, Ryan, I promise."

She came forward again, pulled him down so she could kiss his cheek. He felt about ten years old. Like a kid being praised for getting good grades when, in fact, he'd made a counterfeit report card.

"It'll be the best wedding ever."

He hoped for her sake it was. Ryan remembered too late that Sam was nearby and he stared right at Ryan as he frowned.

"You care to tell me why you look so glum?"

Ryan shook his head. "Wedding nerves."

Sam held his gaze. "Why do I have the feeling there's more to it than that?"

Because they'd known each other forever. "Come on." He clapped Sam on the back. "Let's move those pipes."

Before Sam started probing in earnest...and got the truth out of him.

JORIE DIDN'T SEE Ryan for nearly a week. She was grateful for that. Whether he was avoiding her or truly busy, Jorie didn't know. Odelia said something about transporting some horses, or maybe bringing some horses back. Jorie didn't know which. She was grateful for the break. He was about to get married. To a woman he didn't love. What a tragedy.

"Guess what you get to do today?" Odelia asked with a wide smile.

Jorie could only guess. So far her days had been filled with answering phone calls, investigating other wedding venues for price comparisons, scheduling appointments, and most important of all, overseeing the design of the lakeside venue.

"What's that?" Jorie asked, noticing that her message light was on. Odelia had a state-of-the-art phone system. Jorie had learned she could page anyone within earshot of the ranch all with the click of a button.

"Laurel is taking Ryan into town to register for their wedding."

"Register?"

"There's a store in town," said Odelia excitedly, her gray hair looking mussed today. "It's called Viola. Very trendy. Laurel wants to register there, and I'm sending *you* to help her out."

Jorie's stomach fell toward the region of her toes.

"Wow." She swallowed, trying to think of a diplomatic way to extricate herself from the situation. "I'm really flattered you think she needs my help, but I have the sod contractor coming today. He needs me to mark out the edge of the lawn we want to put down. And then there's the general contractor building the gazebo."

"All taken care of," said Odelia, her smile nearly as bright as the rhinestones on her hot-pink shirt. "I'm taking care of it. I could use a day out in the sun. I've been spending far too much time in my office lately."

Because they had so much to do. Word had gotten out the Spring Hill Ranch had stepped up their game. The web redesign had gone live two days ago and the phone had been ringing off the hook. Jorie didn't know what they'd do when they started advertising.

"Mrs. Clayborne, please, you don't have to take over for me. I'll call Laurel. Tell her to go without me."

"No," Odelia said sharply, so much so that Jorie

found herself going still for a moment. "I specifically told Laurel you would go along."

She was her boss. Someone she'd come to admire. Even so, she knew when it was time to do as she was told.

"What time do I have to meet them there?"

"Eleven."

That meant she had three hours to get some work done. "What's the name of the store again? I'll get directions from Google."

Odelia's smile was radiant. "Thank you, Jorie." But then it faded a bit. "I don't know what's going on with those two. I had them over for dinner the other night and it was like being in a dentist's office. In Ryan's present frame of mind, I wouldn't be surprised if he picked out dishes and linens in black."

Jorie looked up quickly.

"I'm counting on you to keep them from each other's throats."

"Were they arguing?" Jorie asked, and for some reason her heart was pounding.

"You know, I wish they had been. The two of them hardly looked at each other." Odelia pursed her lips. "I'm worried about them."

"I'm sure it's just prewedding jitters."

Odelia shook her head. "I've been around enough brides and grooms to know what that looks like. This isn't it."

Were they breaking up? Was Ryan regretting his decision? And why did Jorie's heart take flight at the thought?

"I'm sure they'll be fine."

Liar. If the cracks were showing now, those cracks would turn into fissures before too long.

"I hope you're right."
"I hope so, too."
Liar, the little voice whispered again.

Chapter Fifteen

"I'm so sorry to have to drag you away from your work," Laurel said. "I know how busy you've been."

Ryan resisted the urge to groan. He hadn't been busy, he'd been avoiding her. That's why he hadn't wanted to run into town with her to pick up some things, but Lyle had insisted.

He hit the brakes a little too hard as he pulled to a stop in front of Viola. "Sorry," he muttered.

What happened to their friendship? Dinner the other night had been painful. He was almost certain his mother had put two and two together.

"I actually have a confession to make." Laurel glanced over at him. "We didn't come to town to pick something up for my dad."

"We didn't?"

"We're here to register for our wedding."

He shut off the engine, but the silence that settled around them seemed to have more to do with what remained unspoken than the quiet of the motor.

"I know you said no, that it wasn't necessary, but your mom talked to my dad and the two of them decided it needed to be done. Only I knew you wouldn't want to do it and so I just made up the excuse of having to go into town. Your mom knows, though."

"Laurel—"

"She insisted Jorie meet us here to help us out."

Jorie.

"I hope you don't mind."

Mind? Of course he didn't mind. This was yet one more nail in his coffin. Why should he mind?

"If it's any consolation, I don't want to do this any more than you do," Laurel said, opening her door and slipping outside before Ryan could say another word. He rested his hands on the steering wheel, watching as she crossed to the front of his truck, sunlight reflecting off his black paint job.

"Son of a—"

He hadn't wanted to register for a reason. Registering meant wedding gifts—gifts they might have to return if they didn't go through with this, but that was looking less and less likely.

"Shit."

Reluctantly, feeling as if he suddenly weighed fifty tons, he slipped out of the truck, the Texas humidity back in full force after last week's rain. It was back to smelling like asphalt and old tires. He hated that smell. City smell.

"There she is," Laurel announced.

He didn't want to look in her direction. He really didn't. Ever since their trail ride he'd been thinking about her. Thinking about her too much.

"Hey," Jorie called as she walked up to them.

Against his better judgment he looked into her eyes, struck once again by their beauty. She wore an ivory-colored blouse—a color she was fond of, he suddenly realized—one that shimmered when she walked and set her skin aglow. One of her long, shapely legs peeked out at him thanks to a thigh-high slit in the ankle-length, beige skirt that she wore. She looked as elegant and chic as a politician's wife, but he knew it was all just an act.

Funny. He couldn't have said what Laurel was wearing today without looking.

"Sorry I'm late," Jorie said, shooting Laurel a smile.

"We just got here, too." Laurel turned, hooked an arm through his own. "No worries."

And it was as if she underwent a change. In front of Jorie, Laurel suddenly seemed exuberant. She flicked her long hair back over her shoulder as she swung back to face him. "Come on, Ryan. Let's go have some fun."

Fun? Had she suddenly taken a happy pill when he wasn't looking?

He hung back, waited for Jorie to acknowledge him. She didn't. All she did was walk past him, and Ryan was left with a good view of her upswept hairstyle and the way the skirt hugged her bottom. She smiled down at Laurel, but completely ignored him, leaving Ryan to wonder if the sweet scent of cinnamon that he caught came from her or the store.

"Goodness." Laurel paused near the door, still holding on to his arm. "It's beautiful in here."

When Ryan glanced down at her, he caught a glimpse of the engagement ring he'd given her and his mood worsened even more.

"Okay," Jorie said. "I've taken the liberty of printing out a list of items that you'll need. One for each of you."

She passed two sheets of paper to Laurel who then handed one to him, Jorie reserving one for herself. Ryan glanced at the list, his stomach tightening.

Linens. Fine china. Appliances.

"Does this store carry all that here?" he asked.

"Of course," said Laurel. "Your mother tells me this is the best place in town to register for a wedding."

The only place in town.

He peered around them, at the china cabinet along the left wall, appliances and home hardware to his right, all sorts of girlie-looking fabric stuff in the middle. Home decor spotted throughout the store.

He glanced at the list again. "We don't need half of this stuff."

The words escaped him before he could think better of it. Jorie finally met his gaze.

"Oh, but you do," she said.

"Maybe if I didn't already own a home." Ryan tried to hand the list back to Jorie. She wouldn't take it. "But I do and I already have all this."

"Yes, but that's *your* stuff," Jorie said, clearly impatient. "This is your chance to pick out items *together*."

Laurel was glancing between the two of them, eyes wide. He waited for her to say something. She didn't.

"Whatever," he said.

You're being an ass.

Maybe he was, he told himself, but Laurel was suddenly acting as though this was a real marriage. As if they had every intention of sharing a bathroom and a bed. All because of Jorie's presence. Did she sense Jorie posed a threat to her? Was that what was going on?

"Let's start with the china first," Jorie said.

China? Were they going to entertain? He supposed they were. Was that before or after Laurel told everyone she was pregnant...with Ryan's baby?

"Do you have any idea what kind of color you'd like?"

Laurel's arm tightened around his. "I don't know, Ryan. What do you think?"

He was thinking he needed to get out of here. That what had started as an offer of help had turned into a monster of a commitment that had begun to make him feel trapped.

"Jorie," he said, "can you give us a moment alone?"

Jorie glanced between them, her stunning blue eyes nearly the same color as one of the dishes behind her. "Sure."

The moment she was a safe distance away, he turned toward Laurel. "Laurel, what's gotten into you? You're acting like a love-struck bride."

Laurel glanced behind him, toward Jorie. "What? You think if we both act like we're about to swallow a vial of plague that it won't get back to your mother? Why do you think she wanted Jorie to go along?"

She had a point.

"I don't want people buying us gifts." He scrubbed a hand over his face, lowered his voice. "Not when all this is temporary."

Laurel's eyes were wide and unblinking, and much to his surprise, suddenly filled with hurt. She looked away for a moment, toward the china.

"Ryan," she said softly. "I know you don't really want to marry me, but can we at least pretend...for my father's sake." She blinked. "And your mother's. At least when people like Jorie are around?"

Her words hit him hard as they were meant to do. Any other woman and he'd think he was being manipulated, but not Laurel. She didn't have a manipulative bone in her body. She was just being Laurel. Trying to please everyone.

"How long?" He didn't even know he was going to ask the question until the words were out of his mouth. "I need to know, Laurel. How long are we going to pretend?"

"I've been thinking about that, Ryan," she whispered

back. "Thinking about what you said by the creek. I agree. Trying to make this work, to see if this might become a real marriage, I can tell that's not a good idea. So just until the baby's born. I promise, Ryan. Once that happens we'll tell my father—"

"Tell me what?"

They both jumped. Laurel turned toward the voice before crying out, "Daddy!"

Lyle Harrington, all six-foot-four-inches of him, stared down at Ryan. He might be dressed like a cowboy in his light blue shirt and pressed jeans, but he looked like a drill sergeant with his stern, angular face and no-nonsense eyes. His gray hair was covered by a black cowboy hat.

"Mr. Harrington." He swallowed back a curse, having to work hard to conceal his dismay. "What brings you down here?"

Lyle Harrington had had Laurel late in life. She was his only child which might explain why he doted upon her. The Harringtons had been neighbors of the Claybornes since before Ryan was born. He'd always looked up to the man, literally. When his father died, Lyle had been there, stepping in as a surrogate father. As such, Ryan had been on the receiving end of a stern word or two more than once in his life. He still felt the aftereffects of that strict upbringing, which might explain why Ryan glanced toward Jorie—guilt causing his cheeks to heat up—as if Lyle had caught him with a girlie magazine under his bed.

"Daddy," Laurel said. "I told you I'd handle this."

"I know, I know," Lyle said. "But I want to make sure it's done right."

"That's why Odelia sent along Jorie," Laurel said.

"Jorie," she called out. "Come tell my father how much we need you here today."

Lyle turned toward Jorie, and Ryan knew the man was not blind. Jorie looked stunning today. Ryan saw Lyle's gaze scan Jorie. He glanced back to Ryan, then back at Jorie again, and his look seemed to say it all.

Fox in the henhouse.

"Nice to see you again, Mr. Harrington."

"Hmm, yes," Lyle said, still studying her. No doubt doing the same thing Ryan did when he'd first spotted her outside the store. Observing the pale blue eyes, the narrow waist, the unique thickness of her naturally blond hair. Lyle turned back to him, brows lifted, his look seeming to say, "Better watch yourself, young man."

"Daddy," Laurel said. "Ryan and I were just talking about china. Do you think we should get something formal, or more country? I really like the plates with the little chickens."

And there she went going back to the happy bride again.

"I like those, too," he heard Jorie say. "They'd be perfect for a farmhouse."

Ryan hung back. He watched as Jorie guided Laurel through the process of choosing wedding gifts. She did so with kindness and firmness, giving her opinions no matter if they contradicted Laurel or Lyle. Occasionally he'd give some input, but he couldn't get over feeling like a hypocrite. They were deceiving Lyle and he hated it as much as he hated deceiving his own mom.

"What do you think?"

They were in the back section of the store, and Ryan was abashed to realize he had no idea what Laurel was questioning him about. But then he saw the bath towels she held, one with a horseshoe embroidered in the middle and one that was plain.

"Plain," he said quickly.

She frowned. Lyle glanced over at him as if disappointed that he'd let down his little girl. Jorie pretended not to notice him standing there.

"I think that about does it," said Jorie, consulting her list and checking something off.

"Terrific," Laurel said. "Who's up for a bite to eat?"

"Not me," Ryan said instantly. "I have work to do back at the ranch."

"Too busy to spend time with your bride?"

Here it went. He'd been giving Lyle a wide berth for exactly this reason. He was so close to his daughter, Ryan had known he'd pick up on the strain between the two of them. Throw in a sprinkle of Jorie, and Ryan knew he was in trouble.

"Not at all," he said, squaring off against him. He would not let the man push him around, no matter how much he respected him. "I promised Mr. Milton I'd deliver some steers to him this afternoon."

Lyle didn't look convinced.

"I have to get back to the office, too," Jorie said, smiling at the three of them. "But thanks for the offer, Laurel." To his surprise, she came forward and gave Laurel a hug. "I hope you get everything you wish for."

Ryan stiffened, wondering just what, exactly, that was supposed to mean.

"Nice to see you again, Mr. Harrington," she said. Ryan watched as she wiped her face of expression before turning in his direction. "I'll see you back at the ranch."

Would he? Somehow he doubted it. She'd done well

at avoiding him in the past week. So had he for that matter.

"Ryan, before you leave, I'd like to have a word with you," Lyle quickly interjected.

He almost groaned.

"Come," the big man said. "Walk with me."

Ryan felt about six years old. He caught a glimpse of Jorie on his way out of the store, her skirt swishing around her legs as she headed to her car. He hadn't meant to look at her. His eyes were naturally drawn to her. Unfortunately, Lyle noticed his glance.

"That's exactly what I wanted to talk to you about," the man said, following his gaze.

"Mr. Harrington—"

"Don't try to brush me off," he said with a wave of his hands. "Look, son. I've known you a long time. I know you have an eye for a pretty girl. And I'm not going to lie, so did I years and years ago. But it's something you grow out of, especially when you get engaged."

"It's not like that."

Lyle held up a hand. "Laurel told me you've been a little standoffish lately."

She'd told him *what?*

"You wouldn't be the first man to have his head turned by a pretty woman a few weeks before his wedding."

"Lyle, it's not like that."

Lyle's lids lowered a bit, as if he studied him thoughtfully. "I sure hope not, but I'm here to tell you that if it is, you need to stop it. I don't want to see my Laurel's heart broken."

It already *was* broken, Ryan wanted to cry out.

"Thank God she had the sense to drop that no good

Thad before it was too late. And thank God you had the good sense to step up to the plate right after. Now all you need to do is see this thing through to the end."

"Yes, sir," Ryan choked out.

"Attaboy," Lyle said, clapping him on the back.

Chapter Sixteen

"How'd it go?"

The words were called out to Jorie from within the arena, and she paused by her car door. Inside she could make out the shape of a figure on a brown horse. Odelia. She trotted up to the rail, her pink outfit matching her fancy pink hat and matching boots.

"It went well," Jorie said. "Laurel picked out some beautiful items."

She heard Odelia tell the horse to walk, then pointed the animal toward the rail, tipping her pink cowboy hat back as she approached Jorie. Her expression was one of concern.

"And Laurel and Ryan?" she asked. "How did they seem to be getting along?"

Fantastic, unless one knew what to look for, Jorie thought. Ryan had tried to appear interested in Laurel's choices, but she could clearly see the sharp edge to his smile. And the way he could barely look into Laurel's eyes…it broke Jorie's heart. The way he'd hung back, too, only showing interest when he was forced to do so. Clearly, Ryan was a man who felt obligated to honor his word, even more so with Laurel's father around.

Lyle.

Now, there was a man who would intimidate a four-star general.

"That well, huh?" Odelia pulled on the reins of her horse, the animal snorting in protest, as she stopped nearby.

"No, no." Jorie closed the distance between them, the shadow of the arena swallowing her up. "It went fine."

"Jorie." Odelia rested her hand on the saddle horn. "You've been working in my office for over two weeks and I can already tell when you're giving me a load of hooey."

Oh, great.

"Lyle called me while you were on your way back to the office. Told me he was concerned about the kids. Frankly, I am, too."

"I'm sure they're just nervous about the wedding."

The horse she rode shifted beneath Odelia, the woman handling the animal with a grace Jorie could only admire.

"Maybe." She frowned, shifted her hat again. "Then again, maybe not, but I've decided to test the waters a bit. I'm throwing them a party this weekend. An engagement party."

Jorie didn't know why her heart sank, but it did.

"I was thinking we could use it as an opportunity to introduce you to everybody, too. So while I could use your help getting stuff together in time for the weekend, you'll be a guest on Saturday night."

She felt as though she'd swallowed a rock. "How many people?"

"No more than thirty. We need to invite everyone in the wedding party. The Harringtons, of course. The ranch staff. Maybe even some of our neighbors."

"I see."

"Formal dress," Odelia added, eyeing the outfit Jorie wore. "Although don't get me wrong. I like that you're wearing jeans more often."

She had worn them. Twice in the past week. She hated it. They'd had three visitors to the ranch and Jorie had felt underdressed the entire time. Maybe Ryan was right. Maybe her clothes really were her armor.

"I'd still like to ride for another half hour, so if you wouldn't mind, I'd love for you to get started calling some caterers. See if anyone's available on such short notice."

"No problem."

"Don't mention the party to Ryan, though. I'll break the news to him."

News he wouldn't like. Jorie was certain of it.

She didn't have much time to dwell on the matter, however. There were six messages on her voice mail when she returned to the office—three potential brides, Sophia, the bride who'd booked the meadow for the spring, and two contractors.

She spent the rest of the day returning phone calls and tracking down the caterers Odelia wanted, most of whom were booked. When Odelia returned to the office, she went over menu choices, then had to call everyone back. The following day was no better, but Jorie was grateful for the work. Odelia put her in charge of personally calling people on her guest list. Though it was short notice, the majority of people could attend, and so from there it was just a matter of getting everything else settled.

And so, one day blended into the next and before she knew it, Saturday had rolled around, her day off, but she found herself working just as hard. For the first time since going to work at Spring Hill Ranch she went up to the great house, as she'd taken to calling Odelia's home. If the place had looked stunning from the outside, it was breathtaking on the inside with its vaulted ceilings, hardwood floors and wall-to-wall windows.

"You go, dear," Odelia told her, coming into a kitchen the size of the mobile home where Jorie had grown up. She'd just met the caterers there. "You need to get dressed."

"Actually, I was thinking I could wear this." She motioned to her capri pants and button-down shirt.

Odelia eyed her up and down. "Excuse me? The queen of fashion wants to wear that to an engagement party?"

"What's wrong with it?"

"You look like you're ready to go wine tasting. I said formal dress, dear, and in Texas, we mean formal."

"Okay. Got it."

Jorie took it as her cue to leave when Odelia assumed her tasks. She walked back to her house, but as always happened, she tensed when she crested the knoll overlooking the old homestead. Ryan's black truck was absent. She breathed a sigh of relief. All week long she'd dreaded running into him. Tonight she would have no choice.

Maybe it was the thought of seeing Ryan again, or maybe it was Odelia's orders to dress formally, but for whatever reason Jorie took extra care with her appearance. She wore a black V-neck shirt, one made to hang off a shoulder and that required a chemise beneath. Both the shirt and the chemise hung past her waist. She belted it with a tiny gold chain. Beneath that, she wore black slacks, but they were fitted with crystal appliqué on the back pockets and around the cuffs and had cost her a fortune. For the first time since arriving, she left her hair down, something she hated to do because it always seemed to get into her face. She applied more makeup than usual, too, stepping back from the mirror when she was finished and wondering if she'd overdone it.

To hell with it. She didn't have time to wash it all off.

She decided to drive up to the house, mostly because she didn't want to destroy her heels, but before she set off she glanced at Ryan's house. He was home. She hadn't even heard him arrive, but she wasn't waiting around to see if he wanted to share a ride.

The sun was just going down, the sky the color of an Easter egg that'd been dipped in orange and blue and pink. Odelia couldn't have picked a better day for a party and it looked as if most everyone they'd invited had decided to attend. Jorie was forced to park down Odelia's driveway a bit. Crickets had begun to chirp, the soft strains of music filling the air.

"There you are," Odelia said, her smile warm and welcoming as she opened the front door.

Jorie had a glimpse of Laurel standing in the corner of a massive dining room to the left of the entryway, Lyle nearby. To the right was a family room, also packed with people, their voices blending in with the sound of classical music. Even as crowded as it was, the place took her breath way. Odelia had painted the walls a deep maroon and off-white crown molding framed the ceiling, fancy molding with lines and squiggles. All the doorways had arched entries, but the arches were filled with half circles of frosted glass, the letters *SPH*—Spring Hill Ranch—etched into the surface. Rattan furniture filled the family room area, the kind with huge round backs and fluffy cushions and lots and lots of plants in between. During the daylight hours it seemed to perfectly blend in with the nearby trees. Earlier, Jorie had wanted to sit there and simply admire it all. She'd never been inside such a gorgeous home. Yes, she'd seen her fair share of opulent residences, but this wasn't garishly done. This was still a home—a beautiful home.

"Did you need something to drink?" Odelia asked.

A double vodka straight-up.

"No, I'm okay," she said instead.

"Well, if you change your mind," said Odelia, looking very Jackie-O tonight in her black dress with a giant broach near one shoulder, "we've set up a bar in the back room, just past the staircase. I'll be back in a bit to introduce you around."

"Thanks," Jorie said softly, happening to glance at the door as Ryan entered.

"And there's my son," she heard Odelia say. "Finally," she muttered under her breath.

Ryan's eyes scanned the room, found hers. He wore no cowboy hat, his face so tan his blue-green eyes stood out even from a distance. This was the first time she'd seen him out of jeans, the black slacks he wore hugging his masculine legs, the white dress shirt emphasizing his masculine arms. Jorie lost her ability to breathe. One second. Two. Who knows how long their gazes would have held if not for Sam stepping between the two of them.

"You're gonna have to do better than that if you want to convince people there's nothing between the two of you."

It took Jorie a moment to follow his words, Sam staring down at her the whole time.

"What?"

The man with the long braid of hair and the kind

brown eyes merely shook his head. "Ryan told me Lyle ripped him a new one the other day...over you."

"Me?"

"Seems he picked up on the fact that Ryan can't keep his eyes off you."

Her cheeks warmed to the point that she knew he could see it. "I don't know what you're talking about."

Sam smirked. Jorie fidgeted. Over the sound of the music came the sound of Laurel's laughter. They both turned to look. Laurel was smiling at something her dad said, Ryan having moved to her side.

It struck her out of the blue, a flash of jealousy so deep it made Jorie physically ill.

"I need a drink."

"I'll go with you," Sam said.

"That's okay. I can bring you something back."

She had a hard time identifying the look in Sam's eyes. "Are you kidding? I'm not leaving your side tonight." It was amusement, she suddenly realized. "Every man in the room is staring daggers at me. I kind of like it."

"Not true," she said quickly. She hated when men said things like that. It always made her so uncomfortable.

"It is true." He smiled. "Besides, I told Odelia I'd keep you company tonight."

"Oh."

"Come on," he said, moving next to her and placing a hand on the small of her back.

The rest of the night went by in a blur, Jorie remembering only snippets of conversation. Odelia found her at some point. She took her away from Sam, introduced her to people Jorie would never remember later. At one point Jorie was handed a champagne glass, her hand tightening around the stem when she realized what was happening. Sure enough, Odelia tapped the sides, the crowd quieting as she toasted the happy couple.

Happy? Jorie thought.

Ryan looked about as happy as a man on his way to jail. She hadn't seen him smile once, not that she'd been watching him that closely. Oh, no. After Sam's warning, she'd made sure to steer clear even as she wondered if it was true. Had Lyle said something? She'd seen the two of them talking outside Viola as she'd been driving away from the store. Had they been talking about her?

"To the happy couple!" Odelia called out to the crowd. Jorie had been so lost in thought she'd missed the entire speech. When it came time to toast, she threw back her glass and chugged the contents in a single gulp.

"Easy there, Cinderella," Sam said quietly.

"I need some fresh air."

She moved away, setting her glass down on the nearest available surface, caring little if Sam, her shadow, followed or not. She was there as a guest, but she'd never felt more of an outsider.

As it turned out, Sam didn't follow. She left through a side door and found herself alone on a portion of the wraparound porch that overlooked the back of Odelia's property. She walked along the rail, finding a spot far away from prying eyes. Earlier in the day she'd been enchanted by the view. The lawn stretched all the way down to the edge of a creek. To her left the bridal cottage stood, soft light spilling from its windows.

Would Laurel get dressed there?

She bit her lips, shook her head, tried to focus instead on the beauty of her surroundings. Portions of the lawn were lit by yard fixtures, tiny blobs of light dotting the perimeter. In the middle of it all sat a kidney-shaped pool. The water looked cool and inviting. There must be speakers outside. Jorie could hear the music perfectly, the strains of a piano concerto soothing her frayed nerves.

"You've been ducking me all night."

She knew who it was, didn't need to turn, her hands clutching the railing.

"I haven't been ducking you."

He came up next to her and it was like being next to a giant magnet, one that tugged at the hairs on her arms and made her feel almost dizzy.

"Yes, you have," he said. "And it's for the same reason why I've been ducking you, too."

She shouldn't ask. She knew she shouldn't, and yet she heard herself saying, "And why is that?"

"Because I can't stop thinking about you."

Chapter Seventeen

He knew he shouldn't be outside with her, knew he should stay by Laurel, yet he couldn't seem to stop himself when he'd watched her slip outside.

"Ryan—"

"No," he said. "Let me just say what I came out here to say."

She stared straight ahead, her profile softly lit by the tiny lights outside.

"I can't stop thinking about our kiss, Jorie. I know I should forget about it. Know I should forget about *you*, but I can't seem to help myself."

"I should go back inside," she said, trying to turn away.

He caught her hand before she could flee. "I promised Laurel I'd be faithful, but damned if I can keep my promise."

"Ryan," she said again.

He knew he shouldn't do it. Knew it went against everything he'd promised Laurel—Laurel who stood inside, no doubt pretending to laugh and enjoy herself, although as miserable as he was inside. Maybe that's why he pulled Jorie toward him. Just one moment of happiness. One moment to pretend everything was all right. She'd driven him crazy all damn night. That outfit she wore. The sexy way it exposed her shoulder... He leaned down, did what he'd fantasized about doing all night, kissed the bare skin that shirt revealed.

"Ryan."

He didn't dare kiss her lips, knowing that if he did, he'd lose himself in the taste of her, lose his control. Instead he placed butterfly kisses upon the line of her collarbone, wanting, craving, needing to have her.

"Oh, Ryan," she moaned.

He found the line of her neck next, dragging his tongue upward until he hit her lips. He heard her gasp. Ryan knew he could have her, knew he could lead her away someplace and she'd follow.

He didn't dare.

His teeth found her ear. He nibbled it, licked it, suckled it and she groaned all over again. It was all he'd allow himself to do, this slow torment, the exquisite taste of her, the touch of his lips against her soft skin. He felt her shift, felt her arm move, her hands slip between his arms and pull him up against her. He leaned back, sucked in a breath.

They hugged.

That was all they did. Ryan felt her heart beat through his shirt. His own heart raced just as quickly. He breathed in the scent of her, tightened his arms, closed his eyes. He could have held her all night. Could have been happy just doing that.

He shouldn't.

"Damn it." He stepped back. "This is crazy."

"I'm sorry," he heard her say.

She was sorry? It was *his* fault.

"I think we should stay away from each other in the future."

She was stepping backward, away from him, her

silhouette slowly fading away. He let her go. He *had* to let her go.

He turned and clutched the rail, breathing deeply until the scent of her disappeared. Lord, he didn't think he could do this. Watching her go back inside had been hell.

"It's Jorie."

He jerked around, surprised to see another silhouette in the darkness. "Laurel," he said softly.

She stepped forward, some of the lighting from the lawn catching her face and illuminating her disappointment.

"My dad mentioned how pretty she was, how she could be a distraction, but I didn't think…"

He lifted his hands. "I swear. All we've done is kissed."

"You kissed her?"

He wasn't going to lie. "The day we got engaged. I kissed her. That was the only time."

"And what do you call tonight?"

He turned and clutched the rail. "Temptation."

"Wait," Laurel said. "You kissed her the day we got engaged and she's still talking to you?"

"She understands."

Laurel laughed, but it wasn't a laugh of amusement. It was amusement tinged with bitterness. "You're sorely mistaken if you believe that."

"No, she does." He scratched at his forehead. "I told her everything, Laurel. She knows you're pregnant. Knows it's Thad's child. Knows our engagement is a sham."

"It's not a sham."

He whirled. "Yes, Laurel, it is. Don't pretend it's not."

There was sufficient light for him to see her shake her head. "You promised you'd try and make this work."

"Yes," he said. "I did."

"At least until after the baby's born."

"And I'll abide by my promise, Laurel. I will. I just saw Jorie here tonight, saw her with Sam, saw them talking and I—"

"—got jealous," Laurel finished for him.

"Something like that."

"You couldn't keep your eyes off her."

He winced. If she'd noticed that, Lyle probably did, too. Crap, his mom might have noticed, too. She'd been frowning at him all night.

"It won't happen again."

She sighed. He could clearly hear it in the darkness. "And if it does?"

"It won't."

She grew quiet again. Ryan thought about going back inside. What more was there left to say? He'd blown it. Big-time. Laurel had caught him red-handed. Maybe he should leave until the day of the wedding.

And what about after the wedding?

"Damn," he muttered.

"Maybe we really should call the whole thing off."

"What?"

"Ryan, you're not the only one bothered by all the lies." She turned to face the lawn, resting her arms against the white railing. "I never expected this to turn into something so big. First the engagement ring. Then shopping for gifts. Now this darn party. I've been try-ing to tell myself it's no big deal, but it *is* a big deal, especially when my fiancé is in love with another woman."

"In love?" he huffed. "Laurel, don't be ridiculous. I hardly know her."

"I hardly knew Thad."

"And look where that ended."

Once the words were out, he wished them back. He didn't want to hurt Laurel, but he knew his observation had to sting.

"I'm sorry," he said quickly. "I didn't mean that the way it sounded, but the thought of Jorie and I being in love, it's silly."

"Only if you don't believe in love at first sight."

"Okay, how much champagne did you consume?"

She'd been standing next to him but she turned to face him then, a hand touching his arm. "I don't know if you're in love with Jorie or not. Like you said, who am I to be the judge? But I *do* know I'm finding it harder and harder to look my father in the eye. It kills me to lie to him. The other day he asked me about Thad and I had to tell him I broke up with him."

"Yeah, he mentioned that to me."

"And now this thing with Jorie." She shook her head. "I feel like I'm Alice gone down the rabbit hole. The deeper I go, the worse it gets."

"I feel the same way."

She was quiet again. For some reason, Ryan held his breath.

"I don't think I can do this."

"Frankly, I don't think I can either."

It was a big, stupid mess. "Yeah, but confessing the truth to my dad scares the crap out of me."

"Me, too." He waited a heartbeat, hoping she'd say the words, and when she didn't he said, "But we have to do it, Laurel."

He didn't think she'd agree. Felt disappointment slide

through his insides. But to his surprise, a moment later she replied, "We have to break it off."

"We do," he said softly. She'd come to her senses. Thank God she'd come to her senses.

"He's going to be furious," Laurel said. "Especially when he finds out I'm pregnant."

"Just as long as he knows I'm not the father."

She bristled. "Of course. I'll tell him that's why I broke things off, because I couldn't stomach marrying you when I was carrying another man's child. He'll understand."

The relief he felt was so great his legs nearly gave out. Only then did he admit how much he'd been dreading his marriage, how much he'd been hoping she'd let him go.

"Thanks, Laurel."

"Can I keep the ring for another day? Just for tonight. It might look funny if I go back inside without it."

"You can have the damn ring."

She laughed a little. "I don't want it." He sensed rather than saw her mood grow more serious. "Your mom's going to hate me."

"No, she won't."

He turned to her. She faced him, too. This was how it used to be between them. Friends.

"I'll pay her back for the party."

"Don't be ridiculous. We can afford it."

She stood up on tiptoe, kissed his cheek. "Thanks for everything, Ryan." She stood back. "I'm so sorry I dragged you into this whole mess."

He was sorry, too, but at least she'd come to her senses before it was too late.

"Take care, Laurel."

"You take care, too." She socked him playfully in the

arm. "Now. Go on after that pretty woman of yours. I have a feeling she'll be glad to hear the news."

"You know," he said, smiling, "she just might."

SHE HAD TO leave the party early.

Jorie knew it was rude, knew Odelia would undoubtedly look for her at some point, but she couldn't stomach sticking around for another minute, not when she would have to watch Ryan be there...with Laurel.

So she got in her car and drove back to her house, all the while thinking how ridiculous it was to long for someone she barely even knew. What did she know about him, really, other than that he was a man of his word, and that he put others above his own needs, and that his touch did things to her that she'd never felt before.

"Dumb, dumb, dumb," she said, banging on her steering wheel when she pulled up in front of her place. What she needed to do was throw herself into her work. Maybe if she did that, the yearning she felt—and, yes, her jealousy of Laurel—would go away.

Who was she kidding?

What was the saying? she thought, opening her car door and slipping into the warm night air. People always wanted what they couldn't have, and Ryan would never be hers.

Something pressed against her leg, something that startled her at first until she realized it was the dog Ryan called Brat. The white portion of its coat stood out in the darkness thanks to a nearly full moon, including the tip of his tail, as if someone had dipped it in a bucket of paint, the end swinging from side to side.

"Thief," she told the dog, though she found herself kneeling down next to him nonetheless, stuffing her car keys in her pocket along the way. She'd never had a pet before. Not because she didn't want one, but because her life had never allowed for one. She'd left home at seventeen, started college early, earned a degree in business through sheer force of will while waiting tables at a local diner. She'd opened Wedding Belles on a shoe-string budget, and with a lot of hard work, had made it one of the most successful businesses in town—until the recession hit and took everything away, including the home she'd been saving up for. Nope. No time for a pet, and no place for one, either.

"You have no idea how lucky you are to live here," she told the dog. "To have people to love you and take care of you."

The dog whined as if understanding her words and trying to reassure her.

"My last boyfriend disappeared the minute I lost my business."

A tongue snuck out and licked her hand.

"And before she died, I hadn't spoken to my mom since I was a kid." She scratched behind the dog's ear. "She didn't want to believe me when I told her the man she'd married made a pass at me."

They'd gotten into a huge argument that ended with Jorie realizing that she and her mom had been as different as oil and vinegar. She saw it all so clearly in the moment. Once she'd left she had never looked back, talking to her mom only on holidays and her birthday. It had been better that way.

Lonely.

Yes. It was that, too.

"When I die, I want to come back as a dog and live in a place exactly like this," she told Brat, straightening.

"If you came here, I'd buy you a rhinestone collar."

She froze, wondered for a moment if she was hearing things, or if maybe it was Sam who'd followed her down.

It wasn't. When she turned, the moon she'd noticed earlier revealed his silhouette.

"We've called off the wedding," he said next, moving closer to her. "Laurel has released me from my promise."

She couldn't breathe.

"And the first thing I thought of, the very first thing I wanted to do, was come to you."

She took a breath, then another and another.

In two steps he'd closed the distance between them, Brat trailing at his heels. "I want to be with you, Jorie," he said. The pads of his fingers, surprisingly soft, stroked the side of her cheek. She closed her eyes.

"I want to make love to you." His hand moved up the side of her face to her hair. "I've wanted to do that since the moment I first saw you in your bed, those damn sheets tangled around your legs."

And still, she held silent.

"You have no idea how badly," he said.

No, she had an idea…she felt the same way, too.

"Will you let me?"

Every nerve in her body began to hum. Her heart thudded in her chest so loudly she was surprised he couldn't hear it. But there was no sense in denying it; she wanted him, too.

"Yes," she whispered. "Please, yes."

Chapter Eighteen

He felt like a teenager.

That's what she did to him. She made him think and want to do things that were so naughty, so completely sexy, that his hands shook. And yet…and yet she also made him want to touch her gently, to relish and to savor and to cherish every soft stroke of his hand against her flesh.

"Let's go inside," he heard her say.

He could have taken her right here, on the front lawn, that was the raunchy side of what she did to him. She took his hand. He followed, surprised to realize he was already hard for her, so hard, in fact, he felt ready to explode.

The moon lit the pathway to her front porch. He thought about guiding her to his home, but that would take longer and he was in such a hurry, he didn't have the patience. She had to fumble for her keys which she'd stashed inside her pants, apparently. Her hands were trembling and it took her a moment to undo the lock, although why she locked her door was beyond him. City thing.

"Here," he said, taking the keys from her. He had a hard time focusing, too. He kept replaying their kiss over in his mind, the kiss they'd shared in this exact spot. Knowing he was about to do a whole lot more than kiss her had him trembling, too. Somehow he managed to drive the key home. He all but fell through the door when it swung wide.

"Let me turn on the light."

"No," he said, tugging her toward the bedroom. He'd played in this house as a kid, knew exactly where everything was, and his steps sped up as he reached her bedroom. He told himself to take it slow, but he was beyond the point of reason. Ryan spun her to face him and planted his mouth on hers more harshly than he intended.

She didn't seem to care.

She opened to him instantly, and she was so hot, her tongue filling his mouth so fully, he felt singed from the inside out. Suddenly kissing her wasn't enough. Suddenly he wanted more, far more.

He pressed his body against hers, their two bodies touching center to center, momentarily distracting him. Only the thought of a far more intimate connection, of stripping her out of her clothes and tasting more than her mouth, had him nudging her backward, Jorie stepping out of her heels along the way. He gently clasped her arms and leaned her back until they were both on the bed, Ryan's body momentarily covering her own until he rolled to the side.

"Take your clothes off."

Once again the words came out harshly, but she seemed to understand his need. She'd left her bathroom light on, the knife-edge of brightness allowing him to see the softness of her face.

"My hands are shaking too badly."

She was trying to undo her belt. He helped her. The gold chain fell away with a clink of the links. His hands found her shirt next. He tried to tug it off. She had to lift her back, and Ryan was pleased with how easily it slid off her torso. If it hadn't, he wasn't at all certain he might not have ripped it off her body, but the sight that greeted him soon had him forgetting about the belt and the shirt and how quickly he was moving things along.

She was beautiful.

Her long hair lay spread out around her, the golden strands catching the light and seeming to be set aglow. She still wore her black slacks and suddenly he became impatient to get her out of them. She seemed to read his mind, undoing the catch, then the zip. He helped her slide the silky fabric down her body.

Shit.

She lay there in nothing but her bra and underwear and Ryan found himself marveling all over again. The sight of her smooth, white skin, of her long legs and the breasts that might still be hidden behind a light brown bra, but were so firm and full all he wanted to do was cup them both.

Whoa.

He was starting to think like a Neanderthal, but that's what she did to him. He was dying, absolutely aching, to touch her—everywhere. And to taste her, the thought barely forming in his brain before he was leaning toward her, not to kiss her lips, but her abdomen, the sight of that little triangle of fabric below her belly button teasing him to the point that his mouth began to move lower, and then lower still.

"Ryan," she said, arching toward him.

His fingers nudged the silky fabric down. Bare skin. Smooth, supple flesh that he tasted and licked.

"Lower."

He tipped his head up, surprised by her tone.

"Kiss me...there."

He grabbed her legs, spread them, his mouth finding her hot center. She moved against him, teasing him into taking more of her in his mouth. She wanted him to remove her panties, wiggled in such a way that he knew that's what she craved. He didn't because oddly enough, he suddenly needed to take it slowly, wanted her to want it...want him so badly that he had her moaning and writhing on the bed. So he taunted her, mouthed her soft nub through the satiny fabric until her hands lowered of their own accord and began to remove the fabric. He nudged her hands away, continued his assault, so turned on that his erection felt ready to bust out of his pants.

"Please," she begged.

No.

He didn't tell her that. Instead he held her hands in place as he nudged the silk aside with his tongue, tasting her salty essence for the first time.

He about lost it then, so much so that he didn't trust himself to continue. He moved up her body, Jorie moaning her protest. He placed a hand against her center as a consolation prize, but she batted it away, her hands moving to his slacks.

"Not yet," he said, trying to move her fingers away.

"Yet," she said firmly.

He took the matter out of her hands by covering her body with his own. Ryan stayed in his own slacks because if she were to take his clothes off, there was no telling what he'd do.

Spread her legs and thrust myself deep inside her.

Yes, he admitted. Definitely that.

So he held both of her hands down with one of his own, his other hand moving to her bra and edging it aside. She had breasts that filled his palm, and rose-colored nipples that begged for his mouth. She moaned when he cupped a hard nub with his lips, writhed beneath him when he nibbled the tip with his teeth, groaned when he suckled her.

Somewhere along the line he'd let go of her hands, and Jorie was working the catch on his slacks without him even noticing. As her hands slipped inside and found the hard length of him, it was his turn to groan.

He lifted his head, all but moaning, "You're going to be the death of me if you keep that up."

"That's the point."

She stunned him then by flipping him onto his back. How she did it, he didn't know. One minute he was flicking his tongue over her nipple and the next she was straddling him, her gorgeous blond hair spilling over her shoulders.

"You're going to be the death of *me* if you don't stop tormenting me."

She slid down his legs a bit, jerking down his slacks. He still wore his white button-down shirt, but she didn't seem to care. She wanted him as badly as he wanted her. That much was obvious by the way she slid his underwear down and then promptly covered his midsection with her moist center.

"No."

"Yes."

"There's no need to rush things."

"There's every need in the world," she said. "*My* need."

She thought she heard him laugh. He was driving her crazy with his teasing assault. But the damn man still wouldn't let her have her way with him. No. Instead he rolled her onto her back again. Jorie was unable to keep from laughing, their tit-for-tat lovemaking causing her to feel giddy.

She was happy.

Never in her wildest dreams did she think it would ever work out between her and Ryan. The night seemed like a gift from God, one she should relish. Yet all she wanted to do was speed things up.

Because you're afraid something will happen, something to spoil the moment.

It was the story of her life. But she refused to think about that tonight. *Refused.* This evening it was her and Ryan and the hard feel of his body against her own, the way the rock-hard length of him found her center despite his best efforts.

He groaned.

She lifted her hips, wrapped her legs around him.

"Stop it."

She used the back of her heels to draw him closer.

"Jorie, not yet."

She hit the target, or rather he hit her target square on, a hiss passing through his lips when they connected.

"Do it."

She could see his eyes in the half light, saw the way his lids lowered. He paused for half a second before thrusting into her.

She cried out.

He pulled back. She clutched at his backside, forcing him inside her, but when he drew back out again she couldn't take it anymore. She pulled away for a moment, tugged his jeans and Jockey shorts all the way off, helping him shed his boots and pants and underwear all at the same time. The moment he was free, she straddled him again.

"Jeez," she heard him rasp. "Jorie. What about protection?"

She drew herself up the length of him. He seemed to freeze for a moment, as if contemplating a run for his pants or his wallet or wherever else he might stash his protection, but then he flipped her onto her back, and Jorie's legs wrapped around his hips at the same time he thrust inside of her again.

Crazy. Wild. Wicked.

He pulled out, and then just as quickly pushed back in. She cried out, her moans matching his thrusts until lights sparked behind her eyes as pleasure spiraled through her body. She couldn't breathe, wrenching her lips away only to cry out Ryan's name.

She waited for him to ride the same wave of pleasure, knew he had to be close, but instead of allowing himself release, he slowed down. Jorie's eyes opened in time to spy him staring at her.

"Again," he said. She didn't know what he meant until he said. "I want to hear you cry out again."

"No," she panted, her hands finding the buttons on his shirt and starting to undo them. "It's your turn."

"Again," was all he said.

He kept moving. She spread the edges of his shirt, pulling them aside. He allowed her, seeming to fling himself out of it. Jorie sighed and ran her hands down his chest when he was finally free of the darn thing. And though she could have sworn a moment ago there was no way he could make her climb any higher, she began to fly again. It wasn't as frenetic this time. He seemed to be taking his time, but how he held on to the edge of his control Jorie didn't know.

"Kiss me," he ordered.

She did, but this time he didn't thrust his tongue inside her mouth. This time he slowly captured her lips with his own, his tongue flicking out to swipe at her lower lip. He kissed her gently, softly, sweetly, as if he could have gone on kissing her all night. Her hands lifted. She buried her fingers in his hair, encouraging him to deepen the kiss. He did, his tongue touching her own just as gently as it had her lips. Time seemed to slow. Their rhythm slowed. Jorie felt something stir, something that warmed her insides in a way that had nothing to do with sex.

"Ryan," she whispered against his lips.

His hands found hers, lifting them up above his head. Jorie climbed higher and higher until, once again, she felt the pressure build to the point of pleasure.

"Ryan," she cried out again.

Finally, at last, he let himself go. She could tell in the way his thrusts became deeper, in the way his kiss became wilder, in the way his body moved as one with her own. She wanted to hear him cry out in pleasure, wanted him to climax the same way she had, and she moved her body in such a way as to bring him satisfaction.

"Jorie."

She could hear the desperation in his voice, feel the hardness of his body. She forced his head down to her, kissed him as deeply as he had her a moment ago, thrust her tongue inside his mouth at the same time he cried out. She felt his release. Felt the throbs of his desire. Moaned at the sense of pleasure it gave her, so much pleasure that she climaxed again with such exquisite perfection that she couldn't breathe for a moment.

"Jorie," he said again, softly this time.

He held her. She let him, her heartbeat slowly returning to normal.

"I don't want to let you go," he murmured.

"You don't have to," she said.

He drew back. She met his gaze.

"I *don't* have to, do I?"

She smiled, stunned to find herself in his arms, feeling the things she felt for him. Things that should scare the crap out of her given how short a time they'd known each other.

"Stay the night?" she asked.

He kissed her again, gently, only drawing back to say, "You couldn't get me to leave if you tried."

Chapter Nineteen

He awoke to the sound of snoring.

He felt a smile come to his lips. Good Lord up in heaven, the girl could snore.

Ryan opened his eyes. There was light in the room, and he realized the sun was pretty high up in the sky. A sliver of heat had snuck past the curtains, warming a portion of their bed.

Jorie's bed.

A glance at Jorie revealed she still slept soundly, her mouth slightly parted.

And then she made the sound.

He huffed out a laugh, thinking he'd never heard a more horrendous yet equally adorable sound in his life. How could someone so beautiful make such a horrible noise?

She was on her side, her hair a golden rope that snaked beneath the pillow. She was snuggling her pillow, like a child worn down by a day of exhausting play. That's exactly what they'd done, too, played all night. Ryan smiled and leaned forward, kissing her shoulder. She moaned. She was just as pretty by morning light as in the evening.

Bang. Bang. Bang.

Curious, Ryan slipped out of bed, looking toward

s own house. He straightened when he realized what e noise was, or rather, who was causing the noise.

Lyle Harrington.

The man lifted a fist and banged on the door again. yan could only think of one reason why he'd be doing at, and it had everything to do with Laurel.

He glanced at Jorie again. She still slept soundly. yan crept over to his slacks and pulled them on. His ll phone was in his pocket. He grabbed it, moving way from the bedroom before dialing. She answered n the first ring.

"Why is your father banging on my door?"

He heard Laurel gasp. "Ryan, thank God," she ushed. "I've been trying to get ahold of you all morn-ig."

"What's going on, Laurel?"

"Why haven't you been answering your cell phone?"

Probably because he'd turned the ringer off last ight. He hadn't wanted to be disturbed at the engage-nent party. "Forget why I haven't been answering, vhat's going on with your father?"

Silence.

"Laurel?" he said, his tone a warning.

"You know what I did. We talked about it last night. I told him we broke things off."

"Yeah, so why is he banging on my door?"

"Because I don't think he believes *I* broke up with *vou*."

"Did you tell him about the pregnancy?"

"That's the other thing."

He clutched the phone. "*What* other thing?"

"I don't think he believes Thad's the father."

Ryan just about jumped out of his skin when the pounding started on Jorie's door.

"Why the hell wouldn't he believe that?"

"Because I told him months ago that Thad an[d] weren't sleeping together. He thinks I broke up wi[th] Thad because of you, that you—you seduced me[, I] guess. He thinks I'm covering for you."

Thud. Thud. Thud.

Ryan lowered his voice, turning from the door. "La[u]rel, you need to call your father right now. Tell him h[e] has it all wrong. Tell him the truth. Tell him I'll take [a] damn paternity test when your baby's born—"

"Ryan?"

Jorie stood in the hallway, a sheet wrapped aroun[d] her body, the similarities to the first time he'd seen h[er] standing there striking.

"What's going on?" she asked. "Who's that poun[d]ing on the door?"

"Lyle Harrington."

She seemed to recognize the implications.

"I've been trying to call him," Laurel was saying[.] "He won't pick up."

"Ryan?" Lyle called. "I know you're in there, yo[u] piece of crap. No wonder you broke things off with m[y] daughter. You couldn't keep your piece in your pants[,] could you?"

"Should I answer?" Jorie asked softly.

"No," he snapped. "Don't answer. He'll go away eventually."

"I'm sorry, Ryan," Laurel said. "Just hold tight. He'[ll] calm down soon. I'll explain things to him again, explain how wonderful you've been, what you were willing to sacrifice so I didn't look like such a loser."

He heard footsteps, and both Ryan and Jorie retreated down the hall in time to avoid being spotted by Lyle, who'd crossed to one of the front windows, cupping his hands as he peered inside.

"This is ridiculous," Jorie said. "Why don't we just answer the door? We've got nothing to hide. You broke it off with Laurel."

"Call him again," Ryan ordered Laurel before slamming the phone closed.

"Didn't you?"

The footsteps sounded again. This time it was the beat of Lyle's feet on the steps. Leaving. He was leaving.

Thank God.

"Yes, we broke up last night. That was Laurel on the phone. Apparently, her father doesn't want to believe *she* broke up with *me,* and that she's not pregnant with my child."

"Oh, dear."

Ryan ran a hand through his hair. "It's a damn mess."

Bang, bang, bang.

Shit.

He was back.

Ryan took a deep breath, went to the door. It took every ounce of his willpower to clasp the door handle and turn it.

"I knew you were in here, you dirty son of a bitch."

Lyle's face was like barbed wire and razors, his blue eyes slashing into Ryan's. He tried to push himself into the house. Ryan stayed him with a hand.

"Lyle, I swear to you, it's not what you think."

"How long have you been cheating on my Laurel?" he demanded.

"I haven't been cheating." He glanced behind the man, praying to God his mom wasn't around, too. She wasn't.

"Then what do you call this?" He tried to push his

way past again, as if he needed to see Jorie with his
own two eyes.

"Lyle, I swear to you. I've never slept with your
daughter. This was all an act, the engagement, Laurel's excitement over the whole thing. She didn't want
you to know—"

"Liar."

Ryan knew he wouldn't get through to the man.
Knew he fought a losing battle. There was no talking
sense into him in his present frame of mind.

"I'm telling you the truth," Ryan said. "I just wish
you would believe me."

"You broke my little girl's heart," he said, stabbing
the air with his finger. "She's been crying her eyes out
all morning."

"Not because of me," Ryan said. "I swear to you,
not because of me."

"You damn no good—"

Lyle turned away, as if unable to stomach the sight
of him. His hands clenched by his sides, so tense Ryan
could see the cords of his neck.

"Sir—"

"No," he said, turning back and pointing at him
again. "You make this right with Laurel." He stepped
sideways, attempted to peer inside the house again.
"And you break it off with your mistress."

"Mistress—"

"I mean it, Ryan. Make it right." He spun away.

"But, sir—"

Lyle just ignored him. Ryan took a step, then stopped.
No sense in following.

Jorie touched his arm. He jumped, hadn't even
known she'd moved near.

"He'll calm down," she said as he closed the door.

She didn't know Lyle very well if she thought that. The man's temper was legendary.

"Come on," she said, smiling. Ryan forgot about Lyle for a second as he stared into her inviting eyes. She grabbed his hand, started to tug him down the hall, and even with sleep clinging to her face—she had a skin wrinkle on one side—and her hair mussed, she was the best-looking woman he'd ever seen. "Let's see if we can beat our record from last night."

God help him, he grew instantly hard at the suggestion.

"I'm actually thinking I should head over to my mother's." He glanced toward the front of the house. They both heard a truck start up. "I wouldn't put it past Lyle to go there next, and I'm sure Laurel hasn't told my mom about our broken engagement."

"Do you think Lyle will tell Odelia you were with me?"

He frowned. "I'm certain of it."

She released his hand. "Crap."

"Yeah. Crap," he repeated.

HE DROVE STRAIGHT over once he'd gotten dressed and showered. Sure enough, Lyle's blue F-150 was out in front, and Ryan was half tempted to back it up and high-tail it out of there.

He couldn't do that. Instead he forced his vehicle forward, forced himself to pull to a stop in front of his mom's house. He took several deep breaths before opening the door.

His mother's voice greeted him. "There you are."

He knew Lyle couldn't be far. Sure enough, he sidled up next to Ryan's mom, the two of them standing on the balcony, his mom seeming to lean against the column next to the stairs.

"Lyle has been telling me some interesting things," his mother said, eyes narrowing.

Did he tell you he wants to kill me?

Somehow Ryan doubted it.

"What's this about you and Laurel breaking things off?"

Though his feet felt like anvils, Ryan approached. He peeked a glance at Lyle, nearly wincing at the anger and disappointment he saw in the man's eyes.

"We broke up," Ryan said simply.

"See. I told you so."

His mom glanced at Lyle, a frown wrinkling the skin between her eyes. "Yes, but I can scarcely believe it. We just had your engagement party last night." As if by having that party it was therefore impossible for them to split up. "What happened?"

"He got my Laurel pregnant."

Apparently, Lyle hadn't gotten that far in the story yet because he saw his mother spin. "What?"

Ryan had reached the bottom step of his mother's porch, climbing them two at a time. "No," he quickly amended. "I didn't get her pregnant, Thad did that."

Lyle pointed at him. "So he says, but we all know how much Laurel loves you. She's just trying to protect you, you lying son of a gun."

Ryan shook his head. "Not true."

"If it's not true then why'd you agree to marry her?" Lyle accused.

It killed him to see his friend and mentor with such an expression of loathing on his face. "She was terrified of you," Ryan admitted frankly. "Afraid of what you'd say. When she came to me crying, asking me if

I would help her out, it sounded reasonable at the time. She's my friend," he said, as if that would explain it all.

"And now that you're sleeping with that damn vixen, that Jorie woman," Lyle said, "she's not your friend anymore."

"What?" his mom gasped. *"Jorie?"*

Apparently, Lyle hadn't gotten around to that part, either. "Relax, Mom, it's not what you think."

"You spent the night with *Jorie?*"

"Yes," he sighed.

"Oh, Ryan, don't tell me you've been cheating on Laurel?" said his mom, the morning sunlight making her look older than usual. Or maybe that was just the worry creasing her brow.

"No." He shook his head in exasperation. "I didn't cheat on Laurel, because Laurel and I were never together."

Lyle crossed his arms in front of him.

"Not really," he tacked on.

"I don't understand." His mom worried her bottom lip, something he hadn't seen her do since he was a teen and prone to staying out past his curfew.

"Mom," he said, moving forward and placing a hand on her shoulder. "Laurel asked me to bail her out, so I did."

Gray lashes blinked. "Define 'bail her out.'"

"I told her I'd marry her."

"After getting her pregnant."

Ryan turned toward Lyle, who'd spoken the words. "I did not get her pregnant, Lyle. I swear to you on my life. The baby is Thad's. A paternity test will prove that if you can't find it in your heart to believe me." He took a step toward his longtime friend. "Do you honestly think I would get Laurel pregnant and then ditch her two weeks before our wedding?"

The words seemed to penetrate where nothing had before.

"You've known me my whole life, Lyle."

"You wouldn't, would you?"

He turned on his mother, who'd asked the question. "Of course not," he said softly.

The hand that still rested on his mother's shoulder fell back to his side. "Laurel was in a bind," he repeated. "I thought I was helping her out. And then I met Jorie."

His mom's hand rose to her chest. "Jorie," she repeated.

"But it wasn't just Jorie," he told them both. "It was… everything. Lying to you, Mom. Pretending like we were in love. Lying to you, too, Lyle. It became too hard…for both of us, especially after last night. That's why we decided to call it off, why Laurel told you the truth this morning." He met Lyle's eyes. "I know you two don't believe me, but I promise it's not a lie."

He glanced at his mom, begging her to believe him.

"You can't call the wedding off yet," his mom said.

"Why not?"

"It'll look bad, Ryan," his mom said.

"Who cares what other people think?"

His mom and Lyle exchanged glances. He saw her shake her head a bit, as if silently communicating with Lyle that she didn't know what to think, either.

"I care." His mom looked sad all of a sudden. "This might affect my business, Ryan. Did you ever think about that?"

"You believe me, right?"

For the first time in a long time, his mom looked utterly serious. "Whether I believe you or not, it won't matter. This will look bad. Word will get out about Jorie, about how she broke you and Laurel up, people will talk. No bride will want her near their groom."

"What?" Ryan spun toward his mom. "That's ridiculous."

"It's what people will think." She looked him firmly in the eye. "She'll have to be let go."

"No. You can't let her go. It's not her fault. It's my fault. Okay. Fine. Maybe I shouldn't have jumped into bed with her, but that was my bad decision. Don't punish her for something I did."

"Last time I checked, it took two to tango," Lyle said, hands resting on his knees. He appeared utterly defeated and disappointed.

"Too bad, too," his mom said. "She was doing such a great job."

"Mom. No. You can't let her go. Okay, fine. We won't announce the wedding's off. We'll wait a week or two. Nobody has to know about me and Jorie. We can keep it between the three of us. Don't fire Jorie."

His mom looked pained. "Time will tell if you're telling the truth," his mom said. "But whatever the case, she should never have slept with you, Ryan. That was a poor choice on her part. And on your part. You're my son. I'm her boss. It's a conflict of interest."

And if we're in love? He wanted to ask his mom that very question except he knew if he did, it would freak her out. Hell, it freaked him out.

"Mom. I'm begging you, don't fire her. She has nothing right now, just her job."

"She should have thought about that before she jumped into bed with you."

Ryan leaned back in shock. He'd never seen his mom look so stern. She turned toward Lyle. "Go home," she told him. "Talk to Laurel. Get Thad's number from her. Or maybe see if she has any evidence my son's not the father of her child. Surely she has a text message or two. Everything's got an electronic trail these days. Ask for proof. I think you'll find my son is innocent."

Ryan breathed a sigh of relief. Text messages. Yes. They *would* prove his innocence. "She and Thad exchanged text messages right after they broke up," he said. "They talked about the baby."

He prayed she still had them.

Lyle's gaze shifted between the two of them. "And if it is true?" he asked. "If Ryan isn't the baby's father?"

His mom turned toward him, her expression one of consideration. "I don't know. But one thing is for certain, Jorie is gone. I suggest you refrain from contacting her once she leaves. A woman capable of sleeping with the boss's son might be capable of filing a sexual harassment lawsuit, too."

"Mom, come on," Ryan said, horrified. "Jorie's never done anything to make you think she was like that. Not a thing."

The disappointment in his mother's eyes was obvious. "No, she hasn't." She shook her head. "But I guess I didn't know Jorie very well, did I?"

Chapter Twenty

"I'm *what?*"

Jorie's heart beat so loudly she could barely hear Odelia's words. They were in the office, Odelia having summoned her there only moments ago. When she'd walked in, she'd known something was wrong.

Very, *very* wrong.

Odelia was not sitting at her desk. No, she sat at the conference room table, a file in front of her. Jorie's employment file.

"Fired, dear," Odelia said with a tight smile. It didn't quite work. The smile didn't reach Odelia's eyes.

Fired.

"Odelia, please. This thing between Ryan and me. It just sort of happened—"

"It *shouldn't* have happened," Odelia quickly interrupted. "He was engaged, as far as I know, practically up until the moment you slept with him. Whether it just happened or not, both of you should have known better. Both of you should have thought about what might happen if someone saw you together."

The disappointment in Odelia's eyes tore at Jorie's soul. She liked this woman. Had wanted to impress her. Instead she'd done something that in Odelia's eyes was completely unforgivable.

"Can you give me a week?"

She hated to sound desperate, but she had no place to go. No family. Nothing.

"I'm afraid not."

She waited, though what she waited for, Jorie didn't know. For Odelia to have a sudden change of heart? God to come down from heaven to rescue her? A knight in shining armor?

Ryan.

"I see."

"I think it would be best if you left the ranch immediately. And please stay away from my son."

Were those tears she felt burning her eyes?

"I didn't do anything wrong," Jorie said, lifting her chin. "Your son. He's amazing, Mrs. Clayborne. The most honorable man I've ever met. I'm not surprised he agreed to marry Laurel. He would do anything for the people he loved. But please don't send me away because of all this."

Lord, was that her begging?

Eyes that were usually so kind stared at her harshly. "But he's just a man, dear, one prone to temptation, which is why you must leave. He is engaged to Laurel again."

What!

"Whether they stay engaged, I don't know, but I will not tolerate any hanky-panky between my son and one of my employees."

"Engaged?" she repeated dully.

"Yes, and so you must leave. I will not have him seduced away from Laurel again."

She made her sound like some kind of Jezebel.

"I didn't steal him. He broke up with Laurel before anything happened between the two of us."

"Really?" Odelia said. "You mean nothing happened before that?"

She looked away, unable to contain her blush.

"That's what I thought." When Jorie looked up again, Odelia was standing. She opened the file in front of her, pulled out an envelope. "I took the liberty of printing out your final paycheck. You'll see I paid you through the end of the week even though I expect you to be gone by tonight."

Tonight.

"I trust that won't be a problem?"

She almost laughed. What did she have to pack?

"No," she said, tipping her chin. "It won't be a problem."

"Excellent," Odelia said, stepping forward and handing her the check. "I'm sorry things didn't work out, my dear." And for the first time Jorie saw genuine disappointment in the woman's eyes, and maybe even a hint of sadness. "You've been a big help. I thank you for that."

Jorie's eyes went back to burning again. "Thank you," she said, having to look away.

"But if you expect any sort of reference, you will leave my son alone."

Jorie inhaled a sharp breath.

"I understand."

"Good."

The word was a dismissal, the verbal equivalent of a hand shove out the door. Jorie took the cue and turned away. But when she reached the door, she paused for a moment.

"Ryan is a good man, Mrs. Clayborne. Too good. He worships you. He'll do anything you say, up to and including staying away from me…if you ask him. I know that. It's one of the things I…" *Love.* She swallowed. "*Admire* about him."

Her eyes were really starting to burn now. She had to blink to hold back the tears.

"But, please, don't force him into marrying Laurel."

"What makes you think I would do that?"

Jorie suddenly couldn't swallow. It felt as if a bucket of tears clogged her throat.

"Your pride," Jorie said. "It will look bad for your business and your family if Ryan cancels the engagement, especially when word gets around that she's pregnant. People will talk. You know that and I know that. I'm afraid you'll do something rash—all so it doesn't reflect badly on the family name or business. So I'm begging you, please, don't put your pride in front of Ryan's happiness. A loveless marriage is something nobody should have to endure. I know. I watched my mom marry someone for convenience sake. I don't know if Ryan told you or not, but my mom had me out of wedlock. For years we struggled. But then, when I was six, my mom met Tim. He was a nice man. Too nice. I could tell my mom didn't really love him, but what did I care? I was getting a new dad, and for a while things were great." Jorie shook her head at the memory. "But then things started to go downhill. My mom ended up breaking Tim's heart. It was horrible to watch. Don't consign Laurel and Ryan to the same kind of life."

She turned, pulled on the damn squeaky door, slipping through the opening before she made a complete fool of herself by saying something else, something remarkable, something completely unbelievable.

Don't make the man I love marry someone else.

"JORIE," RYAN CALLED out, sliding through the front door of his home and damn near tripping over the door frame he was in such a hurry. "Wait."

She ignored him, arms crossed, head bowed, her pace increasing as she'd walked toward her home.

No. Not her home. Not anymore.

His mother had fired her. He'd hoped she wouldn't go through with it, but he could tell by the look on Jorie's face that she'd done exactly that.

"Jorie, damn it," he shouted, rushing to catch up to her. "Wait."

He caught her just as she reached the tiny porch, the same spot where they'd first kissed, the same spot where the evening before he'd turned and guided her to their bed.

"Leave me alone, Ryan."

He jumped in front of her, startling her. "Don't. Please. I know what my mom did. Just give me a couple of hours to talk some sense into her."

She'd been crying. The realization caused a physical ache to land near his heart.

"Aww, honey," he said softly. "I'm so sorry."

He tried tugging her into his arms. She wouldn't let him.

"Your mom says you're engaged to Laurel again." She tipped her chin up. "Is that true?"

"No," he instantly denied. "Not really."

"Not really?"

"It's just temporary."

She held his gaze, her blue eyes never wavering as she waited for him to say something, although what, he had no idea.

"My mom. She thought it might be best if we wait to call it all off, at least for a few days."

And still she said nothing. He had the damndest feeling he'd missed the point of the conversation, although just what that conversation was, he didn't know.

"What?" he huffed when all she did was continue to stare up at him.

"Nothing." She stepped around him.

"Jorie, wait." He grabbed her hand. "What do you want me to say?"

She searched his eyes, then shook her head. "Nothing but what's in your heart, Ryan."

"My heart doesn't want you to leave."

"Is that all?"

"Of course that's all."

The smile she gave him was bittersweet with an edge of sorrow.

"Goodbye, Ryan."

"What? Wait. You can't leave. Not like this."

"There's nothing for me here."

"You have me."

"No, Ryan, I don't. You'll do what your mother says. That's the sort of man you are. And don't get me wrong, it's one of the things I admire most about you, but I can see the handwriting on the wall, and I want to leave before that handwriting tears me apart."

"Jorie," he said, amazed and awed. "You're in love with me, aren't you?"

She wiped at her eyes. "Yeah," she said with a shrug. "I guess I am. Not that it matters. You'll marry Laurel because it's the right thing to do. It's what your mom and Lyle want you to do. The both of you—all of you— too blinded by obligation to see what a huge mistake it would be."

"I'm not marrying Laurel."

"Time will tell."

"If you love me you won't leave me."

"Actually, it's because I love you that I will leave you."

He felt his mouth drop open.

She turned away.

"Jorie—"

"Goodbye, Ryan," she said over her shoulder. "Tell your mom thanks for everything." She paused with her hand on the door. "I mean that, too. I've enjoyed working with her. I only wish I hadn't turned out to be such a huge disappointment."

And then she was gone.

Chapter Twenty-One

"Damn it," Ryan cussed a few days later. "Where the hell did she go?"

"Still can't find her?"

Ryan turned toward the door, and saw Laurel standing there. Laurel, the root of all his problems...and still his friend.

"It's like she disappeared off the face of the earth."

"You don't have her cell phone number?"

"It's been disconnected."

Laurel frowned. "Maybe that's because she doesn't want you to find her."

"I know my mom knows where she is. Someone called for a reference the other day, but when my mom hung up, she wouldn't tell me a thing."

Laurel rested a hand on his shoulder. "Maybe that's for the best."

"I'm not marrying you, Laurel."

His friend winced. "And *I'm* not marrying *you.*"

"I should have never let her go."

"No. You shouldn't have, especially since you love her."

He glanced at Laurel sharply. "What makes you think that?"

Laurel laughed, though it was laughter tinged with

sadness. "Only that you haven't been able to think of anybody but her for the past few days. She's all you talk about. You haven't been the same since she left, either. The old Ryan would have meekly complied with his mother's wishes, not tell Odelia to go to hell when she insisted our engagement continue for another couple of days."

He felt bad about that. He really did. But he refused to be dictated by Odelia and Lyle. Laurel had proven the baby wasn't his. She'd shown the two of them the text messages between her and Thad. It'd soothed things over with Lyle, but he had a feeling his mom would be happy to see him marry Laurel. Thank God she hadn't pressured him into doing exactly that.

"What did you want to see me about, anyway?" Laurel asked. "You're not going to tell me to go to hell, are you?"

They heard the sound of a car and Laurel glanced out the window. It was midafternoon, though the sun was hidden behind large, puffy clouds. Looked like rain again.

"That's what I wanted to talk to you about," Ryan said, pointing.

"Who is it?" She peered out the window, only to stiffen suddenly.

"I might not have been able to find Jorie, but I found Thad."

"Ryan, no." Gray eyes shifted to his, so wide she looked frightened for her life. "You didn't."

"I did," he said. "Told him if he didn't get his ass to the ranch I'd drag him down here behind the back of my horse."

"I don't want to talk to him."

They heard a car door open, then close.

"Too late."

"He broke up with me."

"You scared the shit out of him, just like my mom scared the shit out of me when she suggested we stay engaged. You know the next thing she'd *suggest* is that we actually go through with it." He shook his head. "I had to do something."

"So you tracked Thad down and ordered *him* to marry me?" she said, backing away from him.

"As if I have that kind of power," Ryan said. "Turns out, he wasn't such a reluctant father, after all. Turns out all he needed was a little nudge."

They heard footsteps on the stairs. Laurel turned toward the door, for all the world looking like a woman about to be faced with the Ghost of Christmas Past.

The door opened, the damned hinges squeaking so badly Ryan inwardly cursed. One of these days, he was really going to get around to fixing that.

"Thad," she whispered.

The man who'd thrown Laurel over. The man who'd supposedly broken Laurel's heart. The man who refused to marry her took one look at Laurel and opened his arms.

"Oh, my gosh, Thad," he heard Laurel choke out.

"Laurel," Thad murmured. He walked toward her, and Ryan had to admit, he got a little choked up, too, at the look on the man's face. Laurel might have believed otherwise, but here was someone in love. He might have run out on her, but only because he'd gotten scared, and only because Laurel was demanding marriage. He'd admitted as much to Ryan the other day. He didn't have a job, had nothing to offer a woman like Laurel, had thought she'd be better off without him. It hadn't taken Ryan long to convince him otherwise.

Thad had reached Laurel now, arms still open. He thought Laurel might prove to be stubborn, that she might tell him to go to hell. Instead tears rolled down her cheeks, his best friend pausing for only a moment before sinking into Thad's arms.

"And that's how we're going to solve this whole marriage problem."

Thad looked up. "Mr. Clayborne, I can't thank you enough for making me see reason."

"Yes, you can thank me," said Ryan. "You can thank me by leading Laurel down the aisle next week." He placed his hands on his hips. "Instead of me."

"Only if she'll have me." Thad leaned back. "Will you?"

"I thought you were with another woman?"

Thad winced. "I wasn't, Laurel, I swear. I just said that to hurt you. When you told me you were pregnant, that we'd have to get married, it scared the crap out of me."

"And it *didn't* scare *me?*"

"I know," Thad said. "I know. And I'm sorry. I hear I left a mess in my wake."

"You can say that again," Ryan muttered.

"So will you?" Thad asked gently.

"Will I what?"

"Will you marry me?"

Leave it to Laurel not to immediately answer. "You ran out on me."

"Never again," Thad said, swiping a lock of Laurel's brown hair away from her eyes. "Never will I run out on either of you."

She made him wait half a heartbeat long before sinking into his arms and Ryan knew Thad had his answer.

"Congratulations, you two," he said.

They kissed.

Ryan looked away, and when it became apparent things were growing a little too heated, slipped out of the office. He met his mom on the stairs.

"Is that Thad's truck?" she asked, eyes wide.

"It is." He blocked her path.

"What's going on?"

"Thad asked Laurel to marry her."

His mom covered her mouth with her hand.

"Where is she, Mom?"

The hand slowly dropped away. "Where is who?" she asked.

Ryan realized she wasn't being evasive. She was in shock.

"Where's Jorie?"

"Oh, my goodness, Ryan, Jorie."

"Yes, Jorie."

"She's in—" His mom frowned. "Oh, gosh, I can't remember the name of the town."

"Mom."

"Just give me a moment, will you," she snapped, shushing him with a hand. "It'll come to me."

"Soon, I hope."

"Loveless, Texas!" she all but shouted.

"Are you kidding me?"

"Kidding about what?"

"The name," he said. "Is she really in a place called Loveless?"

"Yes," his mom cried. "Are you going after her?"

"Of course I am," Ryan said, about to push past her.

His mom's hand shot out. "Ryan, wait."

He didn't want to, feeling as if he might miss Jorie if he didn't leave right at that second.

"I know I've been hard on you—"

Ryan snorted.

"And that you must be mad—"

"I'm not mad at you, Mom." Ryan tipped his cowboy hat back, scratched at his forehead. He wanted to leave. Now. "Just disappointed. You should never have tried to pressure me into marrying Laurel."

"I wasn't pressuring you. I never once asked that you actually walk her down the aisle. I was simply suggesting you stay engaged."

"For how long?"

"Well—"

"Until the day of the marriage, right? Wasn't that your plan?" he asked.

His mom huffed loudly. "Okay, maybe I was hoping you'd go through with it. Laurel is such a nice girl. She's perfect for you."

"There's only one woman who's perfect for me," he told his mom, and he knew in that instant what Jorie had been asking him last week, the point she'd been trying to make when she'd asked him to tell her what was in his heart. It all seemed so clear suddenly.

She'd wanted him to admit his love.

They held each other's gaze, and his mom looked so sad and lost that Ryan's heart softened. "Oh, Ryan. I am *so* sorry."

"I love her, Mom. I should have never let her go."

She nodded, wiped at her eyes, her voice sounding clogged with tears when she said, "Then go," and leave it to his mom to wave imperiously toward the road.

For the first time that week, he did exactly as his mother asked.

"Eggs with toast, ham on the side, and a cup of coffee. Black," the trucker said, giving Jorie a wink.

"Eggs, toast, ham on side. Got it."

Jorie forced herself to smile, turning on her heel to place the order. If the man slapped her on the ass as she walked by, she'd scream.

One week.

That's how long she'd been at the tiny little truck stop on the outskirts of town, a place that smelled like bacon grease and diesel for a full twenty-four hours a day, and served coffee so thick it was a wonder anyone could drink it.

"Order," she called to the cook, a man as greasy-looking as the burgers he cooked. Funny, she thought, placing the ticket on the spinner. Only now did she realize Ryan had been right. The way she'd dressed before, all those fancy outfits and equally fancy hairstyles, it'd all been an act. Now that she wore an old-fashioned pink uniform, one with a white apron and a stupid matching cap, only now did Jorie admit that clothes had been her armor. Jorie's way of playing dress-up—and pretending not to be the lost little girl without a mom or a dad.

The doorbell tinkled. Jorie's heart stopped for a moment as she glanced up from behind a long counter where she was getting her customer his coffee. Of course, it wasn't him. It was an old man, one with hardly any hair, and raindrops spotting the top of his coat. It looked miserable outside, as miserable as Jorie felt.

As if Ryan would come here looking for you.

In her dreams. Odelia knew where she was, not that she'd tell her son, not right before his wedding. And the wedding was still on. She'd called one of her contacts in Fredericksburg the other day, a stupid thing to do, but she couldn't seem to stop herself. When she'd asked if the Clayborne wedding was still on this weekend at Spring Hill Ranch she'd been told that it was. It was all she could do not to vomit.

Ryan was going through with it. He was going to marry Laurel.

Idiot.

It was such a bitter pill to swallow, it'd been all she could do not to pick up and leave Texas. Except she couldn't. She had no money. No family. No life. Even more sadly, she'd had to use the last of her paycheck for a deposit on a room. A hotel room. One of those weekly places that rented rooms by the hour to women of questionable morals. But, hell, at least it was a roof over her head. It would do until she found something better.

If she found something better.

She walked toward the booths lining the front of the restaurant, rain splashing the glass. The interior of the restaurant, already dark, grew even darker.

"Here you go." She poured coffee into ham-and-egg man's cup. "Did you want cream or sugar?"

"No, but I'll take some sugar from *you*."

Jorie smiled as if amused. She wasn't. She'd heard it all during her first week as a waitress. She was getting good at playing along. It helped with tips.

"Sorry, hon. I'm seeing someone."

"Are you?" a deep voice said behind her.

She nearly dropped the coffeepot.

"Because if you are that's going to make the next few minutes really, really awkward."

Ryan.

Chapter Twenty-Two

The coffeepot began to tip.

"Whoops," Ryan said, coming forward. "Careful."

He looked so good...so *Ryan*. Black cowboy hat, button-down denim shirt, soft green eyes.

"What are you doing here?"

He took the pot from her, set it down on the ham-and-egg man's table.

"You are one hard woman to find, Jorie Peters."

He was here. Like something out of a dream. Here.

"I've been looking for you for over a week."

"Have you?"

"Do me a favor? Next time you leave town, please don't disconnect your phone number."

The whole thing felt weird. Fuzzy. As if it wasn't really happening.

"I didn't disconnect it," she heard herself say. He looked so good, his face sporting its five o'clock shadow, his black hat emphasizing his light green eyes. So handsome.

So not hers.

"They shut it off." She blinked. Told herself to step away. "No payment."

"I would have paid it for you."

She tipped her chin up. "Would that have been okay with your mom?"

"Her opinion doesn't matter."

She turned away, headed toward the new customer. "What can I get you?" she asked, whipping out her order book.

"A menu would be nice," the old man said.

Jorie closed her eyes for a second. "Ah, yeah. Right."

She turned—and ran smack into Ryan's chest.

"Excuse me," she said, trying to step past.

"No," he said quickly. "You're not running away from me again."

She turned on him. "I didn't run away."

"Yes, you did. You were so utterly convinced that things weren't going to work out, that I was going to throw you over for Laurel and my family, that you took off."

"I took off because it was the right thing to do. What your *mother* asked me to do."

"To hell with my mother." His voice grew louder. "She wasn't the one being asked to marry Laurel."

"A wedding that's still on, I heard."

"Yes," he said. Jorie was shocked at how badly his admission hurt. "Only there's been a change in who's walking down the aisle."

"Oh, yeah? Who'd you get to marry her now? Some other spineless schmuck?"

"Spineless schmuck? Is that what you think of me?"

"You let me go."

"Because you refused to stay."

"You could have followed me."

"You're right. I could have."

She blinked, having not expected the admission.

"I should have," he amended, tilting his head back

and scratching at his forehead. "And I've regretted that decision every damn day of the past week."

Her eyes burned. She couldn't seem to breathe, either. There was a look in his eyes, one that caused her heart to flutter.

"I love you, Jorie."

Her eyes closed. She didn't even realize she'd done it until she felt a hot tear escape through her lashes.

"I should have followed you."

She felt his hands on her arms, felt him gently pull her toward him.

"I will follow you now." His arms wrapped around her. "To the ends of the earth."

This wasn't really happening. This was some crazy dream brought on by serving one too many cups of coffee.

"Marry me, Jorie. Marry me this weekend, in our meadow."

"I can't," she said softly. "You're marrying Laurel. I spoke to the caterer this week. They said the wedding was still on."

"I am getting married," he said, hands clenching around her arms. "To you."

She started to shake her head. "I don't understand."

"The wedding's still on, Jorie. Only you're the bride. We'll have to go down and get a marriage certificate. Today. But I figure you won't mind. My mom said she has a dress for you. She pulled some strings with one of her vendors. Everything else is in place. All we need. All *I* need, is my bride."

More tears spilled down her cheeks.

"But what about Laurel?"

"She's getting married, too. To Thad. They're eloping after our wedding."

It was all too much. She couldn't take it. Ryan seemed to sense the sudden weakness in her legs. He pulled her into his arms. She wilted against him.

This was a dream. It had to be.

"I bought you a ring."

She felt him shift, felt him lean back. She swayed when he let her go, reached into his pocket and pulled out a tiny box. The filigree ring he'd picked out all those weeks ago stared up at her from the box. Her hands shook. She knew that because when she covered up her gasp of surprise, she could feel her fingers trembling against her mouth.

"I got you the right one, didn't I?"

He wasn't marrying Laurel. He wanted to marry *her*.

"Jorie?"

She felt his arms wrap around her again, knew then that this was real, that he really was here—for her.

"Marry me, Jorie."

She gasped in a breath. No. It was a sob. She was crying.

"I even fixed those damn squeaky hinges for you. I love you. I don't know how it happened so quickly, but it did. You're a woman unlike any other. A woman I would be proud to call my wife."

"Oh, Ryan."

He leaned back. Or maybe she leaned back. She didn't know. All she knew was that she was suddenly staring into Ryan's eyes, and he was smiling, and then leaning toward her and kissing her.

"I love you," she said. "I thought I was going to die when I heard you were getting married."

"To you," he said gently. "Only to you."

He grabbed her hand. She watched as he began to slip the ring on her finger.

"Will you marry me, Jorie Peters?"

"For God's sake," they heard someone say. "Would you say yes, already? I'd really like a menu."

Jorie looked up, then smiled. "Yes," she said. "I'll marry you, Ryan Clayborne."

"Well, thank God for that," said the old man in the corner.

Epilogue

"You look beautiful."

Jorie turned away from the mirror Odelia had tucked into the corner of her office/dressing room, hoping she was right. She wanted to be beautiful...for Ryan's sake.

"It fits perfectly."

Odelia came up behind her, the same look of uncertainty mixed with sadness in her eyes that Jorie had spied since she'd arrived at the ranch. "I was pretty certain of your size."

"You guessed it perfectly."

The dress was long and deceptively simple. There were no frills, no abundance of rhinestones or pearls, just a simple wedding dress with a tight bodice and a flared skirt that suited Jorie perfectly. She'd left her hair down long, a short veil hanging down to her shoulders.

"It's exactly what I would have picked out for myself."

Odelia stepped between her and the mirror. Her Western clothes were strangely absent today. Instead Odelia wore a classic silk dress, the same color as her eyes, that reached down to her ankles.

The same color as Ryan's eyes.

"Jorie, I know I already said this, but—"

"Shh," Jorie said softly. "There's no need to apologize again."

"I know, but I'm going to do it anyway." Odelia grabbed her arms. "I'm a stubborn old woman, one who thought she was acting in the best interest of her son—and her family." She looked up at her earnestly. "But I hope you know how hard it was for me to let you go."

She wasn't angry at Odelia. Okay, maybe she had been a little bit, but the one thing the two of them had in common was their love for her son. Jorie understood why Odelia had acted the way she had. She'd been trying to protect her son from the machinations of a woman she barely knew. She would do the same thing to protect her child. *Their* children. Hers and Ryan's.

"Thank you, Odelia."

Her hands dropped back to her side, but Jorie grabbed her hand before the older woman could move away. "I hope you know how much I'm looking forward to becoming a part of your family."

Odelia's lips pressed together. The woman's eyes filled with tears. "I think part of the reason why I was forcing Ryan into Laurel's arms was because I always wanted a daughter."

Jorie smiled. "I know."

Odelia clutched her hand. "Will you be that daughter, Jorie?"

It was Jorie's turn to have her eyes fill with tears. "Of course," she said, her voice raw with emotion.

Odelia's hand squeezed hers again, only to release it when they both heard the clatter and jingle of a team of horses.

"They're here."

The carriage. The one that would take her to the meadow where she and Ryan were getting married.

"Ready?" Odelia asked, handing Jorie her bouquet of white roses and hyacinths. The scent was heavenly, the flowers so beautiful Jorie knew she would remember how the sunlight caught the dew on their petals for the rest of her life.

They set off together. Sam was waiting for Odelia at the bottom of the stairs. The ranch hand smiled.

"Ryan's a lucky man," he called up to her.

He was supposed to take Odelia to the meadow in the Mule, but suddenly, Jorie knew what she wanted to do.

"Ride with me," Jorie said, pausing for a moment.

"In the carriage? Jorie, no. You're supposed to ride by yourself."

"Who says?"

Odelia smiled. "It's tradition."

"To hell with tradition." She put an arm around Odelia's shoulder. "Ride with me and walk me down the aisle."

Odelia almost choked, or at least that's what it sounded like. "Oh, Jorie, no. I couldn't."

"Yes," she said firmly. "You can." She smiled. "Ryan would want it that way if he were here for me to ask."

"But, still—"

"I'm not taking no for an answer."

And so that was how Jorie found herself traveling to a wedding in a white surrey drawn by two black horses, the top pulled back to expose a cloudless sky above. How she found herself clutching Ryan's mom's hand on her way to the meadow. How, when they arrived, she found herself being helped out of that carriage by Odelia, and then kissed on the cheek before her veil was lowered.

Odelia clutched her hands. "My son chose wisely," Odelia said, tears in her eyes.

Drat it all, the tears she'd been so good at holding back suddenly fell. Odelia hooked her arm through Jorie's, the two of them setting off. Jorie had yet to look at Ryan. She couldn't bring herself to do it, was frightened that he wouldn't be there.

But he was.

Of course he was, her tall, dark and handsome cowboy standing at the head of the aisle. Behind him the lake sparkled like scattered glitter.

Was it just a few short weeks ago that she'd been imagining her own marriage in this meadow? Wishing. Hoping. Dreaming.

She closed her eyes for a second.

Do you see that, Mom? There really is such a thing as a happy ever after.

Wedding guests Jorie scarcely knew all stood when she and Odelia paused at the end of the make-shift aisle, a runner covering the grassy surface. Wait. That wasn't true. She knew Sam, the poor man off to the side, a look of misery on his face as he was forced to hold four leashes attached to four happy dogs, all wagging their tails as they caught sight of her. Someone—Odelia no doubt—had tied giant white bows around their necks.

"Don't they look cute?" Odelia asked.

They actually looked mortified. "Adorable."

"Ryan told me if you didn't show up, I was to turn them loose on you."

Jorie laughed. The musicians Odelia had selected began the "Wedding March." And if the other wedding guests thought it strange that Odelia led the bride down the aisle, and that none of them really knew that bride, and that just a few days ago Ryan was set to marry Laurel, not by word or deed did they show it. When she walked forward, people smiled, especially one person in particular—Laurel was silently applauding. She clutched the arm of the man by her side, smiling up at him in a giddy happiness. This weekend Laurel, too, would be married and Jorie couldn't be happier for her.

"You made it," Ryan whispered as she came to a stop next to him.

"Did you think I wouldn't?"

He lifted her veil. "I think I'm the luckiest man in the world," he said as he caught a glimpse of her face.

Once again, tears filled Jorie's eyes. "No," she said. "I'm the lucky one."

"We're *both* lucky."

And as Jorie faced forward, she knew he was right, and that she was about to become the happiest woman on earth, and that it was a happiness that would last for the rest of her life.

And it did.

* * * * *

HEART & HOME

COMING NEXT MONTH
AVAILABLE JULY 10, 2012

#1409 AIDAN: LOYAL COWBOY
Harts of the Rodeo
Cathy McDavid

Can Aidan Hart put aside his responsibilities running the family ranch to deal with his surprise impending fatherhood? Find out in the first book of the Harts of the Rodeo miniseries!

#1410 A BABY ON THE RANCH
Forever, Texas
Marie Ferrarella

Abandoned by her husband, Kasey Stonestreet and her new baby move onto Eli Rodriguez's ranch, where the lifelong friends soon become lovers. *But what will happen when Kasey's husband returns?*

#1411 THE RENEGADE COWBOY RETURNS
Callahan Cowboys
Tina Leonard

Gage Phillips has spent his life as a renegade...until he finds out he has a daughter. Add a feisty Irish redhead who's a natural at motherhood and you have a recipe to tie down the formerly footloose cowboy!

#1412 THE TEXAS RANCHER'S VOW
Legends of Laramie County
Cathy Gillen Thacker

Matt Briscoe suspects the attractive artist hired by his father is hiding something from him. Jen Carson has sworn to keep the elder Briscoe's secret—but how can she, when she's falling in love with Matt?

Lively stories about homes, families and communities like the ones you know. This is romance the all-American way!

You can find more information on upcoming Harlequin® titles, free excerpts and more at www.Harlequin.com.   HARCNM0612

REQUEST YOUR FREE BOOKS!
2 FREE NOVELS PLUS 2 FREE GIFTS!

❧ Harlequin®

American ★ Romance®

LOVE, HOME & HAPPINESS

YES! Please send me 2 FREE Harlequin® American Romance® novels and my 2 FREE gifts (gifts are worth about $10). After receiving them, if I don't wish to receive any more books, I can return the shipping statement marked "cancel." If I don't cancel, I will receive 4 brand-new novels every month and be billed just $4.49 per book in the U.S. or $5.24 per book in Canada. That's a saving of at least 14% off the cover price! It's quite a bargain! Shipping and handling is just 50¢ per book in the U.S. and 75¢ per book in Canada.* I understand that accepting the 2 free books and gifts places me under no obligation to buy anything. I can always return a shipment and cancel at any time. Even if I never buy another book, the two free books and gifts are mine to keep forever.

154/354 HDN FEP2

Name	(PLEASE PRINT)	
Address		Apt. #
City	State/Prov.	Zip/Postal Code

Signature (if under 18, a parent or guardian must sign)

Mail to the **Reader Service:**
IN U.S.A.: P.O. Box 1867, Buffalo, NY 14240-1867
IN CANADA: P.O. Box 609, Fort Erie, Ontario L2A 5X3

Not valid for current subscribers to Harlequin American Romance books.

Want to try two free books from another line?
Call 1-800-873-8635 or visit www.ReaderService.com.

* Terms and prices subject to change without notice. Prices do not include applicable taxes. Sales tax applicable in N.Y. Canadian residents will be charged applicable taxes. Offer not valid in Quebec. This offer is limited to one order per household. All orders subject to credit approval. Credit or debit balances in a customer's account(s) may be offset by any other outstanding balance owed by or to the customer. Please allow 4 to 6 weeks for delivery. Offer available while quantities last.

Your Privacy—The Reader Service is committed to protecting your privacy. Our Privacy Policy is available online at www.ReaderService.com or upon request from the Reader Service.

We make a portion of our mailing list available to reputable third parties that offer products we believe may interest you. If you prefer that we not exchange your name with third parties, or if you wish to clarify or modify your communication preferences, please visit us at www.ReaderService.com/consumerschoice or write to us at Reader Service Preference Service, P.O. Box 9062, Buffalo, NY 14269. Include your complete name and address.

Looking for a great Western read?

Harlequin Books has just the thing!

A Cowboy for Every Mood

Look for the Stetson flash on all Western titles this summer!

Pick up a cowboy book
by some of your favorite authors:

Vicki Lewis Thompson
B.J. Daniels
Patricia Thayer
Cathy McDavid

And many more…

Available wherever books are sold.

Saddle up with Harlequin® and visit
www.Harlequin.com

ACFEM0612

Harlequin® American Romance® presents
a new installment in favorite author Tina Leonard's
miniseries CALLAHAN COWBOYS.

Enjoy a sneak peek at
THE RENEGADE COWBOY RETURNS.

The secret to Gage Phillip's happy existence was ridiculously simple: stay far away from women, specifically those who had marriage on the mind.

He put his duffel on the porch of the New Mexico farmhouse and looked around. The rebuilding project he'd taken on for Jonas Callahan was perfectly suited to a man who loved solitude. Gage knew his formula for a drama-free, productive lifestyle was oversimplified to some, especially ladies who wanted to show him how much better his life could be with a good woman. But the fact that he was thirty-five and a die-hard, footloose cowboy only proved his formula was the best choice a man could ever make on this earth, besides choosing the right career and spending hard-earned cash on a dependable truck.

He hadn't always been die-hard and footloose. Fourteen years ago he'd been at the altar, and he'd learned a valuable lesson: marriage was not for him.

His friends were fond of saying he was just too much of a renegade to be tied down. Gage figured they might have a point. Fatherhood had been a late-breaking news bulletin for him about a year ago—what man was so busy traveling the country that he didn't know he had a daughter?

His ex, Leslie, convinced by her parents not to tell him about his child so they wouldn't have to share custody, had made a midlife conscience-cleansing decision to invite him to Laredo to tell him. He was pretty certain she had told him only because she was at her wit's end—and because Cat was apparently fond of making her mother's new boyfriend miserable.

The situation was messy.

"Excuse me," a woman said, and Gage jumped about a foot. "If you're selling something, I'm not buying, cowboy. And there's a No Trespassing sign posted on the drive, which I'm sure you noticed. And ignored."

He'd whipped around at her first words and found himself staring at a female of slender build, with untamable red hair, eyeing him like a protective mother hen prepared to flap him off the porch. Maybe she was the housekeeper, getting the place cleaned up for his arrival. Anyway, she seemed clear that he wasn't getting past the front door. He tried on a convincing smile to let her know he was harmless. "I'm not selling anything, ma'am. I'm moving in."

Who is this woman? Will she let Gage past the front door?

Find out in THE RENEGADE COWBOY RETURNS.
Available this July wherever books are sold.

This summer, celebrate everything Western
with Harlequin® Books!
www.Harlequin.com/Western

Copyright © 2012 by Tina Leonard